Cross

By

T. S. Worley

World Castle Publishing
http://www.worldcastlepublishing.com

World Castle Publishing
Pensacola, Florida

Copyright © T. S. Worley 2011
ISBN: 9781937085858
Library of Congress Catalogue Number 2011934430

First Edition World Castle Publishing August 22, 2011
http://www.worldcastlepublishing.com

Cover Art: T.S. Worley
Editor: Beth Price

Dedication

To Colene Baker-Thanks for the spark
To the one I share my life with-Thank you for looking at
me as if I'd hung the stars
To my brother-You have always been my steady rock
To my mother- Thank you for the writing gene
To my sweet Aunts
To my "Parder" in crime
To all my supportive family and friends

T. S. Worley

Chapter One

Lest he put forth his hand,
And take also of the tree of life,
And eat, and live forever.
Genesis 3:22

It was June 14th and I was twenty-nine and three hundred sixty-three days old the day my life forever changed. I wasn't looking forward to turning thirty. I'd just gotten used to my twenties and I was about to have to say goodbye to them. I didn't know what thirty was supposed to feel like and I wasn't thrilled about figuring it out. To make things worse, I didn't look thirty, or even twenty-five. I looked and felt much younger than I was. And the older I became, the wider the chasm between my age and my perceived age grew. It added to the sense of disconnect I'd already been feeling.

I looked then just as I do now, 5'9" 165 pounds, slim and muscular. My hair is brown and a little unkempt and my eyes are deep green. My grandmother was Cherokee, and to her I owe my best features; high cheekbones, dark skin, a strong angular jaw, and her mischievous, crooked smile all hung well on my boyish face. I was not the home grown all American boy at all. I was more the atypical good-looking guy from some other place.

I wanted to look my age. I wanted to be perceived as my actual age. I was getting tired of having to explain to people that the men in my family aged slowly and that we probably just had good genes.

I had watched my grandfather outlive two wives and spend the last few years of his life alone because he refused to lose another companion. He was vital and strong 'til the day he died at ninety-nine. I remember people saying at the funeral how good he looked, *not a day over sixty* they said. I remember thinking how lonely he was. I didn't mind the thought of growing old. I did, however, mind being one age and looking another. So there I was, twenty-one going on thirty, not knowing how complicated my seemingly insignificant problem was about to become.

I can't remember much of the beginning...the day everything changed, but this is what I do remember. I was hiking. I loved hiking, but not for the scenery or for my health. I hiked aggressively. I loved the agony that came with it. I loved overcoming the pain; pushing through it and getting that Endorphin high that came at the point of collapse.

I was in the Big South Fork recreational area, a less traveled national park on the rim of the Cumberland Plateau in northern Tennessee, sixty miles or so north of where I lived. I was on one of my favorite trails, The Angel falls trail, named for the rapids by which it passed. It snaked along the South Fork River for many miles. The trail bed was soft with few rocks and the mountains that flanked the river on either side kept the sun at bay even on the hottest of days. However, this didn't hold true that day. Instead, it was overcast and raining a soft fine rain.

The dense canopy of trees through which the trail twisted provided nice shelter from the rain. I was wet more from sweat than from the precipitation. The air in the woods carried an earthy, sweet, pine scent. The smell clung to my damp clothes.

I had just reached the head of the trail, which emerged onto the highway. I had to cross it to pick up the trail on the other side. I never heard it coming. It was such a quiet day. I should have, but I didn't. Music was blaring from my headphones at full volume to drown out my thoughts that morning, and I was pushing myself harder than usual. The end of the bridge would have made mile seventeen.

I didn't really feel the pain at first, just the shock of the sudden movement. The sound of screeching tires seemed so distant. I was suddenly thrown into a whirling void where, for a moment, time and gravity lost their hold on me. I remember the intense impact of the earth hitting me. That's how it felt, like I was motionless and this big planet collided with me. I couldn't breathe or think. A million tiny flashes of light flickered in the darkness. "Let's get out of here!" were the last words I heard before drifting into a deep, warm slumber. I was dying.

I had been found in a crumpled heap beside the road by a couple of tourist from the Empire state. There were no cell phone towers in the park, and maybe I'd have died right there if they had left me to call for help. But rather than leave me, they loaded my broken body into their SUV and drove me over the winding park highway to the rangers' station. From there I was air lifted to the nearest trauma center, which was in my nearby hometown of Knoxville, TN.

I have no memories of the trip there. But at some point I came out of a fog just long enough to hear a heavenly voice command, "Get him up to O.R," her tone was rich and warm like golden honey transformed to sound. I couldn't hold on to the sound and I drifted.

I can only remember bits and pieces after that. Sounds mostly, beeps and grinds of IV pumps and bustling sounds of doctors and nurses. Again I heard the voice, the same angelic one from before, and I struggled to wake up. I squinted in the bright light. Slowly the world cleared. And then, there she stood beaming at me with large, wide, friendly eyes.

"There, there, rest, mama will make it all better," she whispered with a thick unfamiliar accent.

This self-proclaimed surrogate mother wore the name Dr. Bhaskar on her lab coat. She was a short, robust woman with bronze skin and a round jovial face. Her eyes were black as coal and sparkled with life.

Before I could form a coherent line of thought the world went dark. I had lost my hold again. Mingled among my twisted dreams and the disturbing images that drifted through my mind were the whispered voices of the nurses caring for me.

"I wonder what he's holding on for." And "I wonder if he has a family?" I found myself awake again. Her dark livid eyes were surveying me intently.

"Can you hear me?" she asked softly. I tried to say yes but I couldn't speak and panic quickly set in. She saw the look of terror in my eyes.

"Be calm child," she said tenderly. "You are intubated. You cannot speak. Blink once for yes and twice for no, "I acknowledged with a slow quivering blink.

"Good!" she said with confidence. "Do you know your name?"

"Yes" I blinked.

"Do you know where you are?"

Two awkward blinks signaled no.

"You are in the intensive care unit at the University of Tennessee Hospital. You were struck by a car and were brought here by helicopter. You had no identification with you and we do not know who to notify. Do you have family?" she asked cautiously.

"No," I blinked.

"Is there someone you wish for me to contact?"

8

As I answered no, I realized no one would be coming to the hospital. No one would be searching for me. I had lost both my parents when I was seven. My grandparents took me in, but now they were both gone. I had distant relatives and acquaintances but I was close to no one, I had isolated myself from everyone. The sudden realization of this saddened me.

"Friends?"

Twice again, I blinked.

"I see. You are alone then." The finality of her words fell heavily in the stark white room.

I blinked once, forcing a tear from my watery eyes. I tried to wipe it away but I couldn't move

No! No! No!! Was I paralyzed, I screamed inside my own mind. I would have hyper ventilated, but the machine at my bedside steadily regulated my breathing.

"Be calm, it will be alright," she caressed my cheek and paused, for a moment her eyes went dull, and it seemed as though her thoughts were somewhere else. Then the twinkle in her gaze returned as quickly as it had gone and she continued.

"It will be alright, but you must trust me."

This was all a terrible dream I thought. None of it was real. If by some chance it were real, then it was all somehow twisted by some sort of medication.

"Will you trust me?" she asked with a hint of urgency in her voice.

Maybe I was just high on morphine. I didn't know anything for sure, but for some bizarre reason I did trust her. I couldn't help it. She wrapped me in motherly warmth as she spoke. I again closed my eyes slowly to signal yes.

A broad smile spread across her smooth, round face revealing her large, perfect, white teeth. "Good."

She pulled a syringe from the pocket of her lab coat. It was filled with a dark fluid, which she attached to the line already infusing the painkillers into my right arm.

While she worked, thoughts of being paralyzed ran through my mind. *How bad was I? Was I going to die?* In my euphoria I was willing to do whatever she asked, or at least I thought I was.

She moved very close to me and spoke softly.

"You should be dead, and your body is damaged beyond repair. It is not my skill or these machines that keeps you alive. There is something special inside you, something that sets you apart. You have probably felt it all your life, but you are incomplete my child. I hold the missing piece. I have that which you lack and I will give it to you freely. I will give you life, I will give you immortality."

She must be crazy! Or I must be crazy, I thought to myself. *I have to be in some sort of psychiatric ward.* I wanted to run. I wanted to scream, but I couldn't move. I was a helpless victim of this charmingly tender, mad, woman.

My eyes were wide with terror as she began pushing the dark fluid into my IV tubing. My veins burned white hot, up my arm and into my chest. There the heat exploded throughout my body like a sun gone super nova. The pain was maddening. Blinding light filled my vision.

"Close your eyes," she whispered close to my ear.

I wasn't aware that they were open. I tried to send the appropriate signal to the appropriate muscles to close them, not knowing if I had and not knowing why I was still listening to her. The burning began to spread through me like lava.

"I need the crash cart in here!" I heard her shout and a flurry of activity ensued.

My heart began to pound violently. The sound of it thundered in my skull. The pain cut through my brain like a hot sword. After a moment, it occurred to me that even though I was feeling pain, at least I was feeling something. Was that good? Then it happened, my heart stopped. I felt

10

chest compressions and the jolt of paddles, but their efforts were in vain. My heart beat no more, but I was still completely aware when the time of my death was recorded. Why was I awake?! Maybe it was residual electrical activity. Maybe I was still lying on the road and my brain had designed this entire scenario.

"Give me a moment would you?" the Doctor asked.

"Yes of course Dr. Bhaskar," a voice answered.

I heard the sounds of footsteps leading away and I sensed we were alone.

"You will sleep soon my child, death will not hold you. They will come for you to take you to the morgue. Do not fear. I will be there when you wake," I heard her whisper before the lights went out.

***

I was sitting on a rock, perched high on a mountain. The old man sat next to me. I couldn't see his face but I knew I loved him and he loved me. He sat gazing down at the clouds as he spoke to me.

"All things must change, David. Even as this mountain will one day become sand and stone, I will change also. And you too must change."

I wanted to tell him I loved him and that I'd missed him, but I couldn't bring myself to say it. I'd never let anyone else in. Not even him.

I awoke in cold darkness. I was confined, surrounded on all sides by unyielding surfaces. I was about to cry out for help when a door opened at my feet. I was pulled from my steel tomb. I jumped off the slab.

"What's happening?!" I shouted.

She took me by the shoulders and smiled the same broad smile, with those same glistening dark eyes. But something was different about them.

It's funny, I still can't put it into the right words to this day, but everything looked different. The world around me was almost too vivid to process. Sounds, lights, and

11

movements seemed too real to actually be real. It was like suddenly being switched from analog to high definition.

"You are alive. You are re-born. But we do not have much time my child. You must do exactly as I say. Listen carefully, if you stay here much longer we will be discovered. I must conceal what I have done. Go before someone sees you. Time is short."

"What have you done to me?" I demanded again.

"Shh... it is okay. You are whole again, but there is no time to explain. You must leave now! Someone will return. There is much to be done. Much is involved here now. Go down the hall to the service elevator. Go up to the ground floor and out the exit by the Emergency room. In the physicians parking lot you will find a black suburban. The keys will be in the ignition. Take it and go to this address."

She handed me a prescription with 101 Emerald Street beautifully handwritten on it. "Go straight there. Please do not stray. Do not delay. It is not safe out there for you now."

I paused for a moment to consider the possibilities of what that might mean. By my reasoning it hadn't been safe before. I was at the door almost instantly, surprised at the speed with which I moved.

"Wait! May I know your name?"

"My name is David, David Cross," I replied, half telling her and half reassuring myself.

"My beautiful David, Run!"

I sprinted down the hall and took the stairs a flight at a time. Outside it was dark. I didn't know what time it was but it felt like the early hours of morning. There under the streetlight, in the parking spot reserved for the ER Physician, sat the SUV. There was a single key in the ignition. A key chain holding a single silver cross dangled from it. I started the engine and twisted the rear view mirror to look at my face. My hair was caked with blood. It was thick and dry and stained my face. I had some faint bruising and a bit of swelling below my right eye but I couldn't find the source of the blood. Over all I didn't look as bad as I had imagined I would.

I needed to get out of here. I put the vehicle in gear and sped from the parking lot. I drove in the direction of home without a second thought. I needed reality. I needed to be home. Surely this nightmare wouldn't follow me. I could re-group there. I could sit in my own living room and try to sort this all out. But I couldn't bear to think of driving the doctors' car to my house. I was still hoping it was all a nightmare. I thought if I could get my car, go home and sleep, when I woke up it would be over.

I had to drive the painfully silent forty miles to reach the lonely road that led to the west side of the park where I'd left my car. In doing this, I had to pass the place where it all began and, just as suddenly, nearly ended. Several miles in, I rounded the curve to the bridge. The headlights fell on the dark blotch where I had lain. "Thank God I'm alive, if I'm alive, "I mumbled. I hadn't spoken to God in the last couple of years and I wasn't really speaking to him then.

I barely slowed as I crossed the bridge and accelerated up the other side of the ravine. Along the way, my thoughts shifted from believing this was a nightmare and doubting my sanity to how beautiful the park looked in the moonlight. I just couldn't accept that this was all happening. I was locked in some sort of euphoria. I had almost reached the parking area when I impulsively decided to go back to the bridge where I'd been hit. I had to see it again. If by some miracle the bloodstains were gone then maybe the rest of this tortured dream would unravel as well.

I turned around in the road and sped back into the park. On the far side of the park, the road was fairly straight and flat. The moon illuminated a long stretch of road ahead of me. The engine was humming along quietly and the sound of the wind whistled at the windows. I was still trying to sort out the events of the day and absentmindedly feeling for a pulse when suddenly I hit something; or rather something hit me hard on the left front fender, causing me to spin out of control.

I came to a stop facing the opposite direction. There was something in the middle of the road, just inside the reach of my headlights. It was on all fours. I didn't know what to make of this creature. It was large, lanky, hairy, and grotesque. It wobbled, shaking its' head as if disoriented. But it quickly fixated on me. The moment our eyes met I was gripped with fear. It was like realizing you'd just stepped on a rattlesnake. It lunged at me spanning the twenty or so yards between us in two great leaps. It landed on the hood of the truck, fracturing the windshield with its hand-like paws. Without thinking, I scrambled out the door into the road. It sprang off the hood, high into the air, its long arms outstretched, poised to ensnare me. Like some Hollywood action scene time slowed or at least my perception of it seemed to.

The beast was frozen above me. Its claws gleamed in the moonlight. An instinctual desire to fight took hold of me and I sprang up to meet the beast in the air as the scene snapped back in motion. I struck him with unnatural force, throwing him back with bone breaking momentum. We hit the ground together in a tangled struggle for dominance, its' massive fangs gnashing only centimeters from my face. I clutched the animals' neck. It clawed at my arms and chest. I squeezed its neck with newfound strength, and with a crunch I felt its spine give way. It writhed beneath me for a moment then went slack. A final breath escaped its vile, open mouth. The stench was unbearable. I pulled myself to my feet. My wounds were deep and long. Hot sticky blood flowed freely as I ran to the damaged SUV.

I can't remember anything of the drive home. I came to my senses as I turned onto my street. It seemed silly later, but I remember worrying about what my neighbors might think. I lived in an up-scale neighborhood. The lawns were manicured, the cars were German, and the kids were, well, kids. I was the only single guy on the block. I had always wanted the family life but this was as close as I'd gotten. I thought the desperate housewives of the neighborhood would surely be watching, so I pulled into the garage and waited for the door to close. Once it was closed, I jumped out and ran into the house collapsing on my couch.

It felt so good to be at home. I loved being at home. I laid there for a moment struggling to hold on to my sanity, which hung by a thread. I remembered my wounds. My chest and arms tingled but they were now smooth and undamaged. Maybe I was hallucinating, I thought. But the rips and stains on my shirt proved otherwise.

As I lay there a deep thirst welled inside me. "I need a drink," I said aloud. I got up and walked slowly to the kitchen and grabbed an ale from the refrigerator. I opened the top and took a long deep drink. The next few minutes were devastating. It was putrid! I spit it into the sink, gagging as I did so. Quickly I turned on the sink to rinse the awful taste from my mouth. It too was the most revolting substance I had ever put into my body and I immediately began retching violently. I fell to the floor and my body began to empty itself. It was a humiliating experience.

Once it was over I lay still on the cool tile floor and tried to regain my composure and gather what dignity I could muster. I pulled myself up from the floor in revolt and made my way to the bathroom, still feeling the unsatisfied thirst grow stronger by the minute. I pulled off the flimsy scrubs the doctor had given me. I turned on the shower and sat down in the stall, letting the steamy water wash over me. The blood from my hair swirled around the drain and I felt faint. "This is bad; this is really, really bad, "I thought to myself.

I thoroughly cleaned myself and stepped out without drying off. I reached over to the mirror above the sink and swiped away the fog. I couldn't see any sign of injury to my face or anywhere else. This isn't possible I thought. I felt nauseous and waves of hot and cold simultaneously washed over me. I grabbed an old pair of jeans and a t-shirt from the laundry and hurried to the door. I threw on my shoes and headed out to the garage.

"What was that address?" In the console I found the crumpled prescription. I jammed it into my pocket, started the damaged car, opened the door, and backed out onto the street. I paused briefly to assure myself that I was still alive, I was not crazy, and I could do this. I drove across town to the address she had given me. I got out at the brownstone addressed 101 Emerald St. I staggered up the walk, feeling the need to vomit lingering close. It was like being thirsty, hung-over, and drunk all at once. The door was opening. I must have knocked.

"I don't believe in werewolves," I stammered as I fainted through the threshold.

Chapter Two

*Therefore shall they eat of the fruit of their own way, and
be filled with their own devices.*
Proverbs: 31

With a single hand and considerable ease, she lifted
my exhausted form from the tile floor.

"Of course you don't believe in werewolves!" her tone
was harsh and vaguely aristocratic.

She held me upright effortlessly as I clung to her like a
drunken prom date. "It's a miracle, "I heard her whisper.

"I'm so thirsty"

"I should say you are. There were reasons for telling
you to come here," she shouted, half dragging me into a
large sitting room.

"That smell!" She exclaimed, the words catching in her
throat.

"You've been attacked! When!? Where did this
happen? David!"

She was alarmed; it was evident as she spoke.

"You know my name?" I whispered, too weak to hold
my own head upright.

The thirst was all I could think about. I felt if I didn't have something to drink I was going to die, again!

"David, answer me! David, were you followed?"

She shook me and my head lolled around like a rag dolls'. My face fell to rest against the graceful nape of her neck. Her alabaster skin was warm, and her blonde silky hair smelled faintly of jasmine. An erotic wave of desire surged through me. I turned my head slightly to allow my lips to brush her neck. I wanted...I needed to drink.

The rushing waves of hot and cold had come back, bringing with them a desperate need to quench my thirst. I clutched her narrow waist and pressed my lips hard against her neck. My teeth ripped into her skin, releasing a flood of life giving blood. I held her tight and drank deep, clasping the wound with ferocity.

"David! No!" she screamed. She broke free of my grip, thrusting me away. A trail of blood ran down her neck into her blouse. I watched the trail as it saturated the white fabric, curving its way down her chest. I was awash in primal lust. I moved toward her, wanting nothing more than to tear open her pretty blood soaked blouse and suck every last drop of blood from her flesh.

"I said No!! Not like this," she screamed. In a defensive move she struck me with both hands in the chest, sending me flying across the large open room. The far wall halted my flight, the old plaster giving way leaving a crater roughly my size and shape.

I slumped to the floor. No sooner than I'd come to rest, she had crossed the floor and pulled me to the tips of my toes. Her outstretched arm held me at bay. My shirt, knotted in her fist, was pressed under my chin. She stared hard. Her eyes were the color of blue sky in autumn and just as cool.

"No one has EVER bitten me! This is NOT what we are!" She released me and I caught myself, my legs now steady beneath me.

"Who are you? What the hell ARE you? What the HELL am I!?" I screamed back. She strode a few paces away from me. Wiping the blood from her neck and examining it.

She turned, facing me. "My name is Ann."

She was feeling for the wounds on her neck, which had already begun to fade.

"I...I'm sorry. What have I done? I don't know what came over me," I stammered as I wiped the blood from my mouth in disgust.

"Well I do," she shouted. "We could have lost you tonight! You should have come here first! No, I should have come for you ahhh!!!!" she roared.

I felt an emptiness in the pit of my stomach. "I'm going to be sick again."

"No David, no you are not. You are never going to be sick again, and now that you've satisfied your thirst, do you think you could manage to tell me what the hell happened out there tonight?"

"NO! You tell me what's going on. Tell me what she did to me!"

"David, listen to me, you were hit by a car. You were taken to the hospital. Sonja found you there. It was destiny David. She risked everything for the chance that it might work. And it did, here you stand the first male Vampire in a millennia."

I suppose I knew it all along, as crazy as it sounded, I wasn't having any trouble accepting her words. After what I'd seen and done tonight, nothing would ever surprise me again.

"But because of your actions we are all in danger. David there are more of them, many more. You have to tell me exactly what happened," she pleaded with her eyes.

"OK. I'm sorry. I left the hospital. I wanted to go home. I got so tired and hungry and I was so confused...I," I struggled to explain.

"I'm sorry too, David," she broke in. "You shouldn't have been alone. It wasn't your fault. Don't be ashamed. It happens to us all. I'm sorry you went through it without guidance. Did it follow you there? How did you escape?" she asked

"I left the hospital and I was on my way home but I doubled back. Then it happened."

"Damn it! It followed you from the hospital. They're watching her," she picked up the phone and dialed hurriedly. While she waited for a connection she rotated the phone away from her mouth, keeping it to her ear, and asked me again how I escaped.

"I didn't. I killed it. It's dead."

She stared at me for a brief moment and then a voice answered on the other end of the line.

"Sonja, David was attacked. No, he's alright. I don't know they must have been watching the hospital. He said he killed one, I don't know. We are talking now. Yes we're leaving soon," she said before ending the call.

"Are you sure it was dead David?"

"Yes," I answered and recounted the events of the attack.

"It was a Werewolf David. Do you understand that? I don't know how you killed it but you can't ever fight them again. You have to run, get away as fast and as far as you can. They hunt in numbers. They aren't mindless animals. I have no doubt that if you hadn't fled they would have caught and killed you,"

"I thought vampires were immortal," I countered.

"Yes and no, you are ageless now. You will never grow old, never fall prey to sickness or disease. You are immortal in that sense. But if they had gotten hold of you they'd have ripped you to shreds and devoured your remains. I doubt you would have survived that."

"What about Dr. Bhaskar?" I asked.

"Sonja will be fine. She is old and wise. You're a child, newly born and just as vulnerable. She has hardened with time. Don't worry about her. We have to go David. We have to go now. I'll explain everything to you in time, I promise. But right now we're in danger," she took my hand in hers and we hurried from the house to the street.

"This is your car?" I asked, admiring the sleek silver Porsche.

"Just get in," she quipped.

I climbed into the little coupe as she sat staring ahead into the darkness.

"Buckle up, they're coming," she fired the engine and tore out of the tight parking spot with tires screaming, sliding the car around to head in the opposite direction with surprising skill. The tiny German rocket surged forward as the wide rear tires gripped the asphalt. Headlights off, we sailed down the street. In the dim amber streetlights behind us I thought I caught a glimpse of a car stopping at the brownstone we'd fled.

"Do all vampires drive with their headlights off?" I asked, nervously gripping my seat.

"I can see well enough. I'm sure your vision has already improved. It gets better with time."

"You can see in the dark?"

"No not really. It's more like you process faster," she replied.

"I think that happened when that thing jumped me. It was like time stopped for a minute."

"That's right. Your mind functions faster. Your reactions begin to quicken."

Suddenly, a pair of headlights appeared in the rear window.

"Damn it!" she said through clenched teeth.

"Who are they?" Why are they following us?" I asked with alarm.

"To kill us, to kill you."

21

"WHY?"

"They're zealots David. They believe they're cursed and we're responsible."

She took a hard left without slowing down. The Porsche drifted sideways through the intersection beautifully, but the headlights were still behind us.

"They're still there. What are we going to do?" I asked.

"We need to get to the interstate. I can't let them get to you. I won't let them hurt you David," she spoke with such conviction in her trembling voice. I knew at that moment she would give her life for me, but why?

"Ann, look!" I shouted. Another car was pacing us. It was two blocks over and running parallel to our course on the empty streets.

"They're herding us!"

She gripped the emergency brake between us and pulled hard. Before we had time to stop she had shifted into reverse and we were hurtling backward at full throttle. The transmission whined under the stress of the turbo charged engine. The car pursuing us careened passed us. She quickly whipped the car back around and headed east.

"Ann, look. The sun is coming up, "I said nervously. She pulled out the tiny cell phone holding it with her shoulder, keeping both hands on the steering wheel.

"Sonja, I can't lose them. We're coming in fast."

I'd seen enough vampire flicks to know that sunrise meant certain death for the both of us, and the tips of the Appalachian Mountains were crowned in orange light.

"Don't we have to get into a coffin or a mausoleum or something now?" I asked nervously.

She smiled a flirtatious smile.

"Do I look like I sleep in a coffin to you David?"

In fact that is the last place I could imagine her. She was beautiful. Her features were sharp, her eyes crisp and cunning. She was graceful and fierce, like the gazelle and the lion all rolled together.

"No, no you don't," I answered. "But what about the sun?"

"The sun won't harm you David, I promise," she assured me. We merged onto the interstate heading toward the airport. We reached 120mph before we got to the end of the on ramp. Traffic was beginning to pick up as people headed out to work the early shift.

"Where are we going?" I asked.

"To catch a plane," she said, without taking her eyes off the road.

"A plane to where?"

"Providence."

"Providence? Rhode Island? What's in providence?" I questioned.

She turned to me and said softly, "Family."

We blew through the north gate without slowing down and navigated our way to a hanger in the rear of the airport complex where the private jets were housed. Outside the third warehouse, a Gulf Stream G650 sat waiting with engines running.

"Let's go, quickly," she said.

I scrambled out of the car onto the tarmac and ran to the jets metal staircase. As we climbed the stairs to the doorway of the jet, I looked back to see the sun cresting the mountain tops. Through my new vampire eyes, it was the single most spectacular sunrise I'd ever seen. It was the kind of natural beauty that compels you to believe in a higher power. And I realized that my entire life had been leading up to the incredible events of the last twenty-four hours, but I couldn't help wondering if I was still one of God's creatures or if I had become something else.

Once inside the aircraft we fastened ourselves in the plush leather seats side by side.

"We're ready," she phoned to the pilot. She nervously watched the window as we taxied to the runway.

I hated flying, especially the takeoff. The first time I flew I was caught off guard by the sudden acceleration. From a distance airplanes, to me, looked like lumbering giants slowly taking flight. From inside the plane I thought it was more like being strapped into a dragster. This time was no better, but once we were in the air I felt like the roller coaster had stopped and I could relax. Ann unfastened her seat belt, stood up, and ran her fingers through her hair as she paced around the luxurious cabin. Closing her eyes, she gently rubbed her temples.

"Are you OK?" I asked.

"Yes, I'm fine," she answered with a smile.

"How are you? Are you alright?" she asked.

"I will be I think. To be honest, I'm not sure how to feel."

"Alright, let's slow down now. We're safe, now we can talk. I'll answer what I can but I had hoped Sonja could be the one to do this. We had planned to get you out of there, but not that quickly. She had to stay behind to tie up a few loose ends."

"Like what, what loose ends?"

"Well, for starters, you."

"What do you mean?" I asked nervously.

"You disappeared from the hospital, remember? Your body, or a body, had to be found. The official story is that your body was mislabeled, lost, and then later recovered in the morgue. You are, for all practical purposes, dead."

"Guess I'm not going to work today then huh?"

"Probably not," she answered with a quick grin. "Where would you be today, to work I mean?"

"Big South Fork. I'm a...I mean for the last few years I've worked as a park ranger."

I thought about how much I had loved being in the park and I thought about lying there on the road.

"Did they find whoever hit me yet?"

"I don't think so David, I'm sorry."

I've heard people say that eyes are the windows to the soul. Looking into her eyes as she spoke, I could see that mortal death hadn't stolen hers.

"No. No, it's OK, it was my fault anyway," I replied.

She broke away from my gaze as if she feared she would give away some hidden thought.

"Anne, why did she do this to me? How did she do this to me?"

"Let's start from the beginning shall we?" her brows furrowed as she spoke.

"Yes," I replied.

"Alright," she said as her face softened.

"We are the creatures from which all vampire stories have originated. And though some of us have behaved monstrously in the past, we are not monsters David. Our history has had dark shadows cast upon it at times. But we have learned to adapt, to manage our needs. We never kill to satisfy our thirst. We have developed the means of supplying ourselves with the blood we need without hunting or feeding.

"How?" I broke in.

"There are so few of us left David, hunted to near extinction. Those of us who remain live among mortals, moving about unnoticed for the most part. Primarily we tend to work in and around the medical profession or remain close to one who does. We've learned to take what we need to survive, but we do no harm," she said as the deep soulfulness returned to her eyes.

"Do I have to drink blood? What if I don't?"

"Then the thirst takes you, and you will drink. You will kill, "I paused for a moment to consider her words.

"You said I was the first male vampire."

"No. Not the first, but the first to survive in a very long time."

"What do you mean the first to survive?"

"There have been other attempts David, but no male has survived the transformation in two thousand years."

"So, you're all women?"

"Yes, we were all female, until now."

"I don't understand! Why? Why didn't they survive? Why did I?"

"None of them had the correct genetic make-up. Their bodies couldn't handle the metabolic change. Do you know what mitochondria are?"

"Uh, I think so. It's part of a cell right?" Recalling biology class.

"Yes that's right. They supply the energy necessary for cellular metabolism. Mitochondria aren't native to the human body. At some point these tiny invaders entered the systems of ancient man, or woman, and shaped human evolution. It is passed on from mother to child, but with each new birth only the mothers' mitochondria are inherited. Follow?" she asked.

"Yeah, I think so. So, you could trace it back daughter to mother back to say...Eve."

"Right," she laughed. "To Eve."

"So was there a vampire Eve?" I questioned.

"Yes David, we believe there was. There had to be a first."

"Do you have children Ann? Are there any vampire babies?"

"No David. We..," she trailed off.

"There are no vampire children. The only children we create are those we bring into the fold, and they are few and far between. We bring new vampires into the world slowly. It takes time, a long time to prepare someone. The shock of the change is often too much to cope with. Even after years of preparation, madness often results. That's why I want to go slowly with you David. I know this must be very, very difficult for you."

"I'm fine, how does it work?" I asked.

"The change introduces a radically, different mitochondria. The female genome allows for the integration of the new mitochondria, but the Y chromosome prevents the process and the host dies. Once in a while during reproduction a male child will inherit both the mother and fathers mitochondria, merging to female strains. This union allows the male host to survive, or so we believed. Sonja confirmed that theory while you were in the Hospital. She knew there was something different about you. She watched you closely; saw your body struggling to repair itself long after she knew you should be dead. She risked exposure just for the possibility."

"I don't understand. Why is it so important? Why did she try?" I couldn't have guessed the significance of the role I had been plunged into, and she wasn't about to chance telling me. It felt like she wanted to protect me from some awful truth.

"Slowly David." As she turned away again I was sure she was hiding something that her eyes might give away.

I stood up and walked around the cabin. "This is a lot to take in Ann."

"What about that thing? Why did it try to kill me?"

"As I said it takes months, years, to prepare someone for the transformation. I can't explain everything to you all at one time. Trust me David," she implored.

I glanced at the place on her neck where I'd bitten her and I felt remorse for the transgression.

"Milk before meat," she whispered.

"What did you say?"

"Milk before meat. It's just an old saying. Let me teach you the basics. Then we can build from there."

I sat back down and closed my eyes. "Alright, I wish we could stay up here for days. It feels good to be locked away in here."

"We still have a few hours," she said optimistically.

"You talk, I'll listen."

Over the next few hours she dispelled most of the myths associated with Vampires. We had already dealt with the notion of spontaneous combustion in sunlight. She showed me the cross she wore around her neck and spoke of her love for God. I was also very relieved to know that stakes through the heart wouldn't be a problem and that I didn't have to fear Italian restaurants.

She took the time to explain what had happened to my body during the change, choosing her words cautiously as she sensed my embarrassment. She explained that there were many unusual things in the world and that, for the most part, people simply denied them or ignored them to keep their own version of reality intact.

She told me the Werewolves were diligent, persistent, and almost professional in their hunt of vampires. She told stories of the many who were lost at their hands, and that they were great in numbers and deeply entrenched in a cult like existence. However, she skirted their origins. I listened and learned. It was easy listening to her. She had an easy smile and a manner of speaking that disarmed me. And those eyes, they were so deep I think I could see back to the beginning of time itself.

"I think I'm getting tired."

"You're young, you'll fatigue quickly if you don't have frequent nourishment. I'm sorry there aren't any provisions on the plane. The flight was arranged hastily but we'll be landing soon. Lie down, save your strength. Come here."

Ann guided my head to her lap as I stretched out on the plush leather sofa. The hums of the engines were soothing and the sun, through the ample window, fell warm on my face. I closed my eyes as she began delicately running her fingers through my hair.

***

When I opened my eyes I was no longer on the plane. I found myself in a small dimly lit room full of earthen pots of various sizes and shapes.

"Come in David," a voice called from the other side of a high shelf, stacked with wares. I walked around the corner to find the old man sitting at a pottery wheel, working a lump of clay. His back was to me, but I knew who he was.

"I made them all," he said as he gestured about the room.

***

The bark of the landing gear tires hitting the runway startled me from my dream.

"It's OK David, we've landed," she said, still stroking my hair.

I rubbed my eyes sleepily. "I've been having strange dreams."

"Dreams? Did you dream?"

Her hand paused mid-stroke. I sat up and faced her, feeling a little dizzy.

"Yes. Why?"

"I'm not sure what that means David. We never dream."

I was beginning to feel the surges of hot and cold again.

"It's happening again."

"Let's get you home," she pulled me to my feet; put my arm around her shoulder and her arm around my waist. "Lean on me. I've got you." We stepped out of the plane in to the bright sunlight. The sky was cloudless and blue.

"There's the car, come on." We walked down the stairs and crossed the short distance to the waiting Mercedes. My legs were beginning to tremble. "Almost there," she assured me.

Once inside the car, an enthusiastic young man in a starched white shirt, black suit, and tie greeted us.

"Welcome back Miss Falen," he said bubbling with excitement.

"Good to see you too, Alex."

"So, is this him?" he asked with un-contained curiosity.

"Alexander! Drive," she scolded.

"Yes ma'am, sorry," he said as he turned in his seat. He put the car in gear and pulled out quickly. I was getting weaker by the second.

"I'm sorry Alex. He's weak. He hasn't fed. We had to leave in a hurry. Get us home please."

"Yes ma'am, I understand."

"Hold on David. We'll be home soon."

I closed my eyes and nestled my face against her neck. My lips touching the place where I had first tasted blood. I was growing restless. The thirst was taking me. I was on the cusp of losing control when she slid her hand gently between my lips and her neck, nicking herself with her fingernail.

"Drink David."

I didn't hesitate. The moment it touched my lips I was lost in ecstasy. It was like a drug. I suckled and lapped the tiny wound, taking what little blood escaped. I relished every drop as she held me in an unyielding embrace. Her nails pressed hard into my strengthening skin. It was a small drink but it was enough to allow me to gather my wits.

"Thank you," I whispered, still resting against her.

She kissed my forehead gently as she whispered, "You're welcome," her tense body now relaxed. I hadn't been this physically close to another woman in quite some time and I felt like I was losing myself to her. Twice now I had drank life from her body. The first by force, and the second time she had willingly shared herself. I felt a deep connection with her now, and it terrified me.

Young Alex glanced frequently into the rear view mirror as he drove. His discomfort was obvious as he shifted in his seat. Never the less, he swiftly navigated the heavy traffic leaving the airport. My mind began to clear and I sat up to have a look around.

"Where's he taking us?" I asked as Alex continued to stifle his excitement.

"To the east side, we're going home."

I wanted to ask where home was, what home was, so many things, but my entire world had just turned upside down. I was struggling to right myself and I didn't feel like playing twenty questions. Besides, I figured I'd find out soon enough.

Providence had an old world look and feel about it, but was densely populated. There were people milling about everywhere. It would be easy to fade into the crowd here, I thought to myself. I was glad we were there. I felt anonymous. I could hardly imagine werewolves, bent on my destruction, strolling around in downtown Providence. We rode in silent comfort for the remainder of the drive.

The sun was high in the still cloudless sky when we arrived at our destination. It was a mammoth old structure. Its windowless facade stood stalwart and unyielding to weather and time. A small moss covered plaque embedded in the old stone humbly read, "The Church of the Lost Shepherd."

"What is this place?"

"This is home."

"It's a church."

"It's our church David, and my home."

"What do you mean *our church?*"

"This is where we worship. This is our church, our vampire church."

"You'll be safe here," young Alex piped in, no longer able to contain himself.

"Listen Ann, this has all been crazy but I think I'm handling it pretty well. And I sense there are things you don't want to tell me because you're afraid I won't be able to handle it. And that's OK but if you're planning on me becoming some kind of un-dead altar boy then I'm getting the hell out of here."

My past had taught me to distrust organized religion or anyone claiming to be of God.

"Oh David! Please don't say such things!" she pleaded, her face was full of anguish. "I'm not trying to convert you into anything. Yes, there are many things you don't yet understand but David I promise you this: I won't ever try to change you. I am asking you again to please continue to trust me."

It went against everything my life had taught me but I agreed to go inside. And so I entered The Church of the Lost Shepherd.

Chapter Three

Her house sinks down to death,
And her course leads to the shades.
All who go to her cannot return
And find again the paths of life.
Proverbs 2:18-19

I hadn't been within the walls of a church since I had
lost Sarah four years earlier. Sarah was the love of my life.
In fact, she was the only one I had ever allowed myself to
love. And if there are soul mates in this life then surely she
was mine. But, as good things often don't, it didn't last.
She walked away from me, broke our engagement, and
severed all ties to me and to her family.

I met Sarah on spring break. A few friends and I rented
a beach house in South Carolina. We were playing
volleyball on the beach one day with a few girls who had
rented the house next door. Sarah was one of them. She sat
on the sand watching us play. I noticed her watching me in
particular. Every time I looked at her she was looking back
at me. Enjoying the attention, I started showing off for her
and she seemed to like it.

After the game she walked up to me and said with absolute sincerity, "I'm Sarah Donovan and I'm going to be your wife."

I fell for her the moment she smiled. She was my kind of perfect. She was beautiful and she knew it, but not so much that it showed. She knew she had imperfections, but she was at ease with them. She was pure, inside and out. I couldn't get enough of her. I spent every second of the rest of spring break with her. We hardly left the room that week and only got out of bed when we had to. After spring break she transferred to UT and we became inseparable. We planned our lives together. We talked about our wedding, our home, and what our children might look like. I felt happy for the first time in my adult life. Life could not have been any better, that is, until Marcus Bennett came into our lives and everything drastically changed.

Marcus came in as a replacement for her religious theories professor. He seemed to take a special interest in Sarah right away. He started spending a lot of time with her after class, and I saw them more than once standing close as they shared whispers in the halls. I tried not to let it get to me, but I couldn't help myself.

When I met Sarah it was the first time I hadn't felt alone. I couldn't stand to think of losing her. And after Marcus, I felt like things were different somehow. Before Marcus we hadn't discussed religion at all, and after he came into our lives it was all she talked about. And not just religion: God, myths, legends, monsters, and the supernatural. It was all I heard, that and Marcus, Marcus, Marcus.

It was a mistake, but rather than lose her to someone else I pushed her away. It's strange how the mind works sometimes, especially mine. I was damaged goods. I had a mortal fear of being abandoned. I couldn't stand to lose her, so choosing to end it seemed the only choice for me at the time. She pleaded with me to stay. She swore there was nothing to fear from Marcus, but my heart told me otherwise. She cared for him. I could see it, so I had to go. I moved out of the apartment we shared and dropped a couple of classes to avoid her.

I loved her so much, but the thought of losing her to someone else was far too painful. I thought I was making the right choice, but when I heard she was leaving town I went into a panic. I went to the apartment only to find that it was empty. The lady next door said she had left for the airport. I suddenly knew I had made a terrible mistake. I had to try and stop her from leaving. I had to explain how I felt and why I had acted the way I had. But when I got to the airport I realized I was right all along when I saw her there with Marcus. They were boarding a plane together. When she saw me standing there at the gate, she just looked back at me. She showed no emotion or expression, with Marcus by her side glaring at me.

I watched her walk out of sight and just like that she was gone. Like a rapidly disappearing dream in the morning light, a vapor, a mist, that I couldn't hold onto. Now it seems as though she wasn't ever really there. I decided at that moment that I was destined to be alone. I vowed to never love another. I blamed God for losing her and for losing my parents. I hated God and I hated church. All of those old feelings came rushing back as I stepped through the door. It was like it had happened yesterday.

Ann must have sensed my apprehension and squeezed my hand. "It's alright David. You are safe here."

The old church had been completely restored or perfectly preserved. The rich mahogany walls and low candlelight soothed me a bit. There seemed to be no one inside save for Ann, Alex, and I. She led me through the vast sanctuary, out the back of the church, and to a small cottage like parsonage neatly attached to the rear of the church. It was cozy and warm. A fire burned in the small stone fireplace.

"Will you be needing anything Mrs. Falen?" Alex politely asked.

"No, thank you Alex. We'll be fine," he slipped quietly out of the room, leaving us to the sound of the crackling fire.

"What now?" I asked.

"We wait. We wait for Sonja."

She crossed the small living area, which was walled with bare stone, to a small kitchen area with stainless steel counter tops. There was no stove, oven, microwave, not so much as a toaster. The only appliance was a small stainless steel refrigerator. "You need to feed again."

She opened the refrigerator and removed a silver metallic cylinder. From the cabinet above the counter she removed a large crystal wine glass. She poured the contents of the cylinder into the glass and carried it to me. She moved so gracefully. I imagined she could sprint through an obstacle course without spilling a drop.

"It won't taste the same," she said. "I mean it won't taste like me, obviously, it's cold and anti-coagulants have been added. They won't hurt you but they do affect the flavor."

I took the glass from her hands and again felt the warmth of her skin. Her touch exhilarated me. I think she felt it too. There was something there I couldn't quite figure out, some sort of connection.

I put the glass to my lips and took a small sip. It was thin, much thinner than her blood, and in addition to the iron taste there was a taste almost like penny's in my mouth. It seemed to vent from my nostrils as I drank. Though it was cold I still got the sudden rush of heat as it spread through my body.

Once when I was young, a friend and I bought moonshine from an old bootlegger on a Saturday night. It was like drinking liquid heat. This was like that except it warmed more than my stomach. I felt it from the top of my head to my toes. I felt more alive than I ever had. My sip quickly became a gulp; I finished the glass with a gasp. "MORE," she laughed with delight.

"What?" I asked.

"David," she said. "Stop breathing."

"What??"

"Stop breathing, you don't need to do it you know, "I followed her direction and at first I felt a slight urge of self-preservation telling me to inhale but I felt no physiologic need to breathe. "You will find that you need only breathe when you speak. We require air to resonate our voices, but that's all. I'm sure you noticed a difference in the sound of our voices."

"Yes I have. Your voice is beautiful."

She smiled humbly. "Mortal voices rise from imperfect vocal cords. The damage begins the day they are born with that first cry. All your wounds have healed David. Every flaw you had is gone. Your body has perfected itself. You, too, now speak with a clear voice."

She poured another glass and I drank it eagerly while awkwardly trying not to breathe. Without breath the metallic taste wasn't nearly as strong. Again the cold fluid generated a warm rush through my body. I started feeling a little euphoric and my eyes rolled a bit.

"I think you've had enough," she cautioned.

"I feel woozy." Am I getting drunk?"

"Afraid so," she said. "It happens sometimes, especially to the young. You have to be careful when you feed. You can lose yourself, David."

That moment in the brownstone flashed into my mind.

"Be mindful of where you feed and how much. And breathe in the presence of mortals," she laughed.

I was feeling warm and cozy. I felt the need to sleep coming on. There was a small bedroom with a large bed filling most of it just off the tiny living room. The bed was beckoning to me. "Come David," she took me by the hand

and led me to the bedroom. It was generously pillowed with soft white bedding over an ample feather mattress. I half crawled into the bed and collapsed under my own weight onto the turned down sheets. She gently slipped in next to me and covered us both with the heavy blankets.

***

I was with Him again. He knelt on the ground digging his hands deep in the rich earth. A great vineyard surrounded us.

"From a single seed," he said as he kneaded the soil with his aged hands.

I expected to wake up after the cryptic message, but instead another voice rang out from behind me. It was crass and challenging.

"Have you grown tired of his foolish riddles? I know I have."

Without looking up the old man spoke again.

"Leave this place."

Chapter Four

When I saw him, I fell at his feet as though dead. Then he placed his right hand on me and said: "Do not be afraid. I am the First and the Last. I am the Living One; I was dead, and now look, I am alive forever and ever! And I hold the keys of death and Hades.
Revelation 1:17

"Tell me everything my child," Sonja said, poised in an old wooden chair at the bedside. "Tell me about the dreams you've been having." Ann was absent from the room but the bed was still warm where she had been laying. Her sweet scent lingered.

"How long have you been sitting there?" I asked.

"Only a few moments. You were restless. What dreams trouble you? Tell mama everything."

I felt a deep trust for her. I would have told her anything she wanted to know. I tried to explain the dreams to her as best I could while she thoughtfully gazed at me with those large brown eyes. She broke in a few times to have me expound on a particular detail, but for the most part she sat silent and motionless until I had finished my report.

"I must consider your words for a time David, for this was something I had not anticipated. You see, we do not dream."

"Yes I know. Ann told me."

"As for now I am sure you have many questions for me."

I sat up on the bed, and pulled a pillow into my lap.

"Who are you?"

"Now that is a question indeed. Who am I?" she paused. "I am the first David. I am she, who is the mother of all vampires. I have walked this earth for eons. I cannot recall my origins. My birth is shrouded in mystery and fog. But I am ancient. I have seen the waters rise up and cover much of the land. I have seen the retreat of ice and snow. I have prowled as a nameless wanderer with beasts that no longer walk the earth. I am, perhaps, as old as time itself. And in my travels I have been known by many names to many people. But to those who would destroy us, I am called Lilith. Do you know this name?" she asked.

"No, I don't think so," I replied.

"This name (Lilith) comes from ancient Hebrew Lore. I must share this story with you. It is said that she was the first wife of the first man, created by God from the same clay from which He created Adam, the first man. Adam demanded Lilith be subject to him, but having been created his equal, Lilith refused to submit to him. So, having no other recourse, she fled from the Garden of Eden."

"Adam in his loneliness cried out to God in despair. And God was angry to find Lilith nowhere in the garden. He sent three of his Angels: Senoy, Sansenoy, and Semangelof to bring her back. Swiftly they caught her by the Red Sea and demanded she return. But she was strong of will and she resisted the Angels. She fought against them and they were forced to return without her. As punishment for her disobedience, God bid her never again to return to the Garden of Eden. Never again to dream the dreams of man, and denied her children."

"It was said that God then made a new wife for Adam. One not his equal, but rather created from his marrow, and together they bore many sons and daughters. Legend says that Lilith too had been with child when she battled with the Angels. And as a result, her child was still born. She was driven mad with grief by the death of her offspring and she began killing the sons of Adam and Eve in retribution, feeding on their life force, trying to fill the emptiness in her soul."

"From the daughters of Adam and Eve she found a way to steal away companions for herself. Created by means of her own blood, she gave rise to creatures such as herself. But God, in his anger, continued to refuse her a son in any form and damned those she created to carry her curse as well," she paused, looking at me longingly.

"Perhaps I was she, David," she continued. "I do not know. But in two thousand years there has been but one other and he was taken from me. I could not save him, not even from himself." For a moment she seemed far away. Her eyes were dull and lifeless. Then she returned.

"What happened to him?" I pressed.

"I will tell you David, but you must give me your word that you will hear my tale entirely."

"Alright."

"Good," she smiled. "As I said before, I have walked this earth for a very long time and I have been many things to many people. I have inspired terror in the hearts of some and have been worshiped as a goddess by others. I have created many of my kind, most of whom chose to end their own lives. Others attempted to create a male numerous times, always with the same outcome. Always the same outcome, that is, until..," she trailed off.

"In 26 AD I returned to the center of the world. I was drawn to the war and unrest of the Near East region. I found myself in the small but bustling town of Natzeret. I passed for human and traveled with absolute anonymity. I needed no food or shelter and I kept to myself. I spent most of my days in the streets stalking my prey, and my nights violently feeding on those I deemed unworthy of the life they possessed. I was, in my own estimation, an abomination."

"It was a dark time in my existence. I had, for quite some time, been consuming any and all written word. I am fluent in many tongues and proficient in most. The vast majority of writings of that time were dedicated to God. Everything I read, with few exceptions, in every corner of the populated world confirmed what I had come to accept. I was truly a creature cursed by God."

"Even there, a thousand years after I had first encountered the name Lilith, were the whispered rumors of *the she demon,* come to take another. A body had been found battered, broken, and bloodless. It was the remains of a man on whom I had fed the night before, his demise attributed to an ancient curse. I no longer cared. The days of mysticism were fading and I no longer desired to stand before a trembling people to be worshiped or reviled. I was what I was, an enemy of the one God."

"On I moved, hunting and killing without fear or remorse. That is, until one fateful day. I was roaming through unfamiliar streets of a town, which had not existed in centuries past. I had crossed this part of the world countless times. Cities were built, conquered, and destroyed in what were mere moments to me. Natzerat was no exception. It was an ever-changing part of the world. Much as it is today. It was mid-morning. The sun was climbing in the hazy summer sky. The people were bustling about haggling in the markets, unknowing that death walked closely among them."

"I was searching for the next one on whom I could unleash the force of my bitterness, a bitterness that I myself did not fully understand, when I noticed a large crowd had gathered in the square. Dozens of people sat and stood listening to a young man speak. He was charismatic and very handsome. I drew a bit closer to hear what it was they were so closely listening to. He was speaking of love, kindness, forgiveness, and making, while professing boldly to be the Son of God. There were some in the crowd who were displeased with his rhetoric, but even they hung on his every word. He was an extraordinary young man."

"I marked this man immediately as my nights prey. I stayed and listened to all he said. I studied his movements. My eyes followed his precisely. I had hunted many beasts and all manner of men. I knew my prey better than it knew itself. But I detected no deception in him. He believed what he spoke. This made me want to destroy him all the more."

"I followed him distantly as he moved about the city. He was surrounded by a swarm of followers wherever he went. People seemed to be drawn to him. As the sun set however, as if upon request, he departed into the wilderness alone. I moved on him, silent and unseen I closed the distance between him and me. As I drew closer, he stopped by a large olive tree. He rested against its gnarled trunk. I could see the whites of his eyes glistening in the light of the moon as he stared up at the heavens. I was about to spring upon him when he spoke aloud."

"Have you come for me? Be at peace, I do not fear death."

"I was enraged at having been discovered. I sprang out of hiding and pounced at his feet. I cannot imagine what a hideous snarling sight I must have been, but again he spoke the truth. There was no fear in his eyes."

"What torments you so, mother? He asked me softly."

"I was dumbfounded. I rose slowly to my feet. I had not the words to answer. I was out of my method. I had not conversed with another in many years and I was terrified. Can you imagine? There I was, ready to tear him limb from limb and I was honestly quaking. He reached with outspread arms and embraced me. I was shocked. I could not recall a time when I had felt the soft touch of another. I had seen humans embrace countless times, but it had never occurred to me to ponder what it might feel like. It was curiously wonderful."

"If you feel you must kill me, mother, share your burden with me first, he implored. His eyes were pained and sorrowful."

"You cannot carry my burden child, I hissed. My burden is death and no man may carry it, God will not allow it. I continued."

"Then I will ask him to allow me to carry it," he said with confidence.

"He was so sincere and innocent, and I was a monster standing before him. I could not bear the interaction any longer. I bolted from his presence with great speed. I had crossed many miles before I stopped. I was distraught. I had images, thoughts, memories, and emotions churning inside me and I was thirsty."

"I set off again, bounding like a wild beast, in search of blood. I soon caught the scent of man. I quickly closed on a camel and his rider. I knocked him from his perch like a great cat and pinned him to the ground. I was about to end his life. I thirsted for the blood he carried in his veins. But I could not do it. The terror on his face wounded me. The scent of the young Galilean also still hung on my clothes, and reminded me of his embrace. I released my victim. Terrified, he ran screaming into the night."

"I turned to his beast and dulled the thirst. But I experienced guilt for what I had done, for assaulting the traveler. I had never cared what they thought or felt. They had always meant nothing to me but in my mind I could feel a great dam beginning to break. It threatened to drown me with memories of the faces and screams of those whose lives I had taken. With but a few words he had affected me profoundly. I had to get back to him. I had to destroy him and thus destroy the turmoil I felt inside."

"I returned to the olive grove in hopes of picking up his trail, but it wasn't necessary. He was kneeling on the ground where I had left him, and I could hear his whispered prayers. He was praying for me just as he said he would, asking God for the strength to carry my burden. I began to weep. Tears of blood streamed down my face. He rose and approached me slowly. His eyes sought out mine in the darkness. He placed his hand on my face and wiped his finger through the trail of blood on my cheek."

"This is what troubles you mother? This is your burden, is it not? He asked."

"It will kill you, "I said.

"God will not allow it," he answered, as he touched the blood to his lips.

"It will be over soon I thought to myself. I felt relief and sadness at the sealing of his fate. In seconds I could see the change beginning. His breath quickened, I could hear his heart race, and then he collapsed at my feet. I knelt to comfort him in his last moments."

"Child, the creature that I am, why did you call me mother?" I asked. No answer came. I wept over him. I wept for his death. I held his lifeless body, mourning the loss of the beautiful human I had not even known."

"Hours passed and I sat motionless in the dark. I wondered if perhaps it was my time to end as well. Maybe I had lived long enough. I had endured so long I wondered if I could die. I have seen my creations die by their own choosing, but none had lived as long as I."

"You have to understand, David. I had not felt anything but bitterness and angst for so long that I knew nothing else. Love, remorse, kindness, and compassion did not exist in my world. One single encounter had changed all of that. The dam had broken. I was sinking. I had actually begun to plan my demise when something caught my eye. The smallest of details do not escape my sight. A shadow had moved in the moonlight in the distance among the trees. The air was still, and I neither smelled nor heard any living thing but I sensed that I was being watched. There had been many times in the past that I had been inadvertently mistaken for prey. But I was yet to know fear. I gently eased the Galilean's lifeless body to the ground and moved silently in the direction of the mysterious shadow."

"There has never been a hunter as skilled as I David, yet I could not discern the source of the movements which seemed always just outside of my range. Something was eluding me. I had pursued it a few hundred meters into the trees when it occurred to me that I was being lured. I was being lured away from the Galilean. I abandoned the chase and returned to find him still lying on the ground."

"Perhaps it is death I thought to myself, my own death lingering, waiting for the right moment to envelope me in shadow. I saw it again moving closer and closer, glimpses of darkness, darting from tree to tree. I waited; ready to strike the moment it showed itself. Closer and closer it moved in silence. Every fiber of my being told me that something as unnatural as I was approaching. It was almost upon me. I would fight and meet my end tonight. I searched the darkness with my keen eyes, but I could not see my enemy. I hissed and roared at the empty night but my calls went unanswered."

"Then I heard the faintest of whispers, leave him, leave him, it urged. The sounds seemed to come from all around me. They grew louder as the moments passed. I turned round and round but I could see no one. There are many strange creatures in this world David but this, I believe, was not of this world."

"On and on it urged, faster and faster, like cicadas in the summer, leave him, leave him. I screamed at it commanding that it show itself. The whispers stopped. Silence fell, not a sound could be heard. The clouds in the moonlit sky were motionless. I felt fear for the first time at that moment. Not from death or injury, but from the unknown. It was devastating for me to think that I had been that very same unknown to so many poor souls."

"Something stirred. Quickly I turned, and to my dismay I witnessed the Galilean rising to his feet. Gracefully he moved. Awestruck, he approached, taking in the world and his own body with large wonder filled eyes. Whatever was lurking in the night had gone. I have come to believe that it knew he would live and did not want me to witness his return."

"Mother," he said with wonderment. "What has happened to me?"

"Oh Child. I cried as I took him in my arms. I could not believe what I was seeing. He had survived. I didn't understand or even care why. He was alive and that was all that mattered."

***

I had given her my word to hear her story entirely, but I couldn't keep quiet any longer.

"Who was he?" I asked.

"David, I know this is difficult, my life changed that night. I had never encountered a being such as him. He taught me to feel love, and more importantly he taught me to love God. He saved me David."

"Who...was...he?"

"David, you know of whom I speak, Yeshua Ben Natzarat...Jesus of Nazareth."

"Stop! No! This isn't right. Don't say that. You're crazy. This is all crazy. It doesn't make sense."

"David, child, you know that I speak the truth."

"I have to get out of here!" I fled out the side door into the courtyard. I didn't know where to go, where to run. So I stood there in the sunlight with my eyes closed. The sunlight seemed to make me feel better.

"David, please don't go, "It was Ann. She had followed me out. I don't know where she came from, but the moment I went for the door she was in right behind me. She made no effort to physically stop me.

"Please stay."

I opened my eyes and turned to her. She was so beautiful in the sunlight. She was flawless, flawless, except for the crimson tears streaking her face.

"Why Ann? Why? Why are you crying, why am I here? Why do you want me to stay? I feel so lost now. I don't know where to go. I don't know what to do. I don't even pray anymore. I don't know if I even believe in God anymore. And she is in there telling me she knew Jesus Christ the Vampire. What am I supposed to say to that, Ann!?"

"I know David, it's a shock. This has all been a shock. Just look at me, look and listen to me. It isn't meant to be this fast. You need time. You need to absorb this slowly. Sonja is telling you the truth."

"I know, I believe her but it doesn't make it easier."

"Come back inside, please."

She took my hand as we walked back inside.

Sonja sat on the bed, smiling warmly with her legs crossed under her. "Come, both of you. David, Lie down and close your eyes and listen. Do not believe or disbelieve, just listen." We made ourselves comfortable on the ample bed and she continued.

"Let us say, David, that I knew a beautiful man who became a beautiful, wonderful immortal who believed that mankind was destined to be something more. More than that, it was the destiny of mankind to gain immortality. It is important that you understand. He saw our kind as the next step in a long path to Godhood. And I came to believe that myself."

"I traveled with him. I became a student of his teachings. I devoted my life to him, such as it is. He became my shepherd. I no longer took human life to sustain myself. It was a struggle, but it was then I discovered that next to human blood, the blood of creatures of the sea was the most satisfying."

"I also began honing my skills as a healer. I had taken so much from mankind that I wanted to spend my existence helping humanity, and having nothing to fear from the diseases that ravaged mankind. We began seeking out the sick and infirm. Word spread quickly. Before long we did not need seek them out, they sought us."

"In time we traveled to the town of Magdala. When we arrived we met a young widow who had been suffering from fever and convulsions. She was very near death and at that time I had a very limited skill set with which to treat her. Her husband had been a fisherman and was killed during a terrible storm at sea. Soon after this she fell ill. She was young, beautiful, and suffering. Her name was Mary."

"He was captivated with her. He asked me to save her. I had not created another in the time we had spent together, and I was hesitant to do so then. But I felt that if I did not, certainly he would. I know now that she was probably suffering from a bacterial infection. But to those in her community she was an outcast who was possessed by demons."

"I remember being frustrated by their mysticism, a vampire frustrated by the superstitions of an ignorant people. It was not easy for her. She was fragile, so very fragile. She had been all her life. The loss of her husband, the illness, and the transformation only worsened her condition. She was ever on the brink of mental collapse and had to be hidden often, as she was prone to weeping."

"He loved her David. He loved her more than anything, and she loved him as well. They were very close. As his ministry grew, so did unrest and contention. I urged him to flee the region. I tried to tempt him with tales of faraway lands beyond the boundaries of the known world, but he would not leave. He refused to abandon his followers, whose numbers were growing exponentially. He felt it was vital to finish what he had started."

"Tensions soon escalated to the point that we had all come to be seen as conspiring criminals, enemies of the state and the religious leaders alike. It was easy to see what was coming. His arrest was imminent. I was ready to protect him from anyone or anything. However, I was not ready for the decision he was about to make."

"We often spent nights walking outside the walls of cities, in the untamed wilderness. We walked hand in hand in silence for a bit, and I was beginning to sense that something terrible was about to happen. After a time he broke the silence, asking that I care for her after he was gone. I knew instantly what he was saying and I protested wildly. It was to no avail. He told me calmly that it was the only way. It was God's plan. He must go as a lamb to slaughter to save humanity. He said that he could accomplish more in death than he could ever hope to in life. He said soldiers would be coming for him and he forbade me to intervene. It was terrible for all of us, especially for Mary and I. We allowed him to be taken, tried like a criminal, and put to death. It was the most difficult thing I have ever endured, watching him there, suffering."

"You have felt the thirst David. Can you imagine what it was like for him? It's one of the few ways we can die, and it is the worst. He was impaled, bleeding, the wounds unable to close. I know he could smell the blood of the others who were also crucified that day in Roman fashion."

"I cried as I heard him whisper, I'm thirsty. Mary had to be taken away. I was afraid she would reveal herself. I remained at his feet. At any moment I would have slain them all and rescued him, but he would not allow it. He suffered all that day but he lingered. The thirst must have been increasingly maddening with each drop of blood he lost. They taunted him, cursed him, spat at him, and yet he loved them."

"The two humans who hung there had died hours before. The soldiers on post had begun to grow uneasy. One of them drew his sword and opened a great wound in his side. It was the end of him. He was gone. I felt my old bitterness returning, I was angry. I took the soldiers' meaty hand in the full force of my grip. He dropped his blade and I felt his fragile bones threatening to give way as he cried out."

"This night shall be your last, I said to him.

Confused and frightened he ran from me, but he could not hide. I had his scent. That night I sat in the darkness outside his home. I had lost my rod, my anchor. I wanted to leave these people and flee this region, lose myself in the north. I was seething with hatred. I was so conflicted. I wanted to take his life as he had taken the life of my creation, and yet I wanted to forgive him as I knew Yeshua had already done."

"Outside the walls of his home I could hear the laughter of his children, the whispers he shared with his wife. He told her about the terrible thing he was required to do that day, and of the strange woman with hands of iron. There was no malice in him. He was not an evil man. He was merely a soldier doing his duty to support his family."

"I could not kill him. I knew I should not be there. I could not run away to the north. I had to stay and protect her as I had promised. I was about to go when a shadow moved in the street. I was frozen where I stood. Again I caught a glimpse as it moved. It was as before. I could not smell or otherwise sense a living presence. It was there and not there at all. It was only a few meters away. I could vaguely discern its outline. It was darker than the night around it."

"Kill him," it whispered. "Kill him, kill him," it repeated.

"I will not, I answered. It uttered a shrill hiss and burst through the soldiers' door, splintering the wood with explosive force. Screams from inside the small home rang out. I ran inside. Two small lifeless, twisted bodies lay prone on the floor. Another scream came from the rear of the home. I ran as quickly as I could to the bedroom, but the voice of the young mother had forever been silenced."

"A dim oil lamp burned in the corner, illuminating the room. The darkness had the soldier. It covered him. He writhed within it. I reached into it. I tried to free him, but my hands grasped nothing. It was intangible, but powerful. It was a demon; an agent of the adversary, and it entered him. It filled him with its vile darkness. His body thrashed on the floor. Guttural screams came out of his torturously stretched mouth. His body was rapidly transforming, snapping, twisting, and growing. He became what you saw last night, David, it was the first werewolf."

"It burst through the wall onto the street. I pursued it but, quick as I am, I had difficulty holding ground. I could not overtake it, and it was heading for Mary. I should have been with her that night. I have wondered so many times what might have happened if I had been there for her. I was only seconds behind it David, but it was long enough. It tore her apart. It ripped through her home and through her without ever halting. She looked away as pools of red liquid formed in the lids of her eyes.

"It was only then that I realized the extent of how grave an error in judgment I had made. She had been with child. I did not know it was even possible."

"Oh, David, I was in despair. My family was gone. I had failed them both. And in doing so I had caused the loss of a new species, a unique creature never before seen in this world. What would the child have been? Was it to be the next step in our evolution as he had said? He must have known she was pregnant. That is what he was talking about. That is why he sacrificed himself, to protect her.

And he trusted me to protect her and his child, my grandchild."

"I am sorry, I need a moment. Please excuse me," she left the room through the door leading back into the main structure. Ann still sat next to me on the bed.

"You said there were no vampire babies Ann."

"There aren't, I didn't want to tell you something she needed to tell you herself. It hasn't been easy for her to go on living. Sometimes I think the struggle is the only thing that's kept her going."

"What struggle?"

Ann was about to answer when Sonja returned to the room.

"The same struggle you fought last night, David. I am alright now. May I continue?

"Of course, "I replied.

"The night Mary was killed. I stayed with her until well after sunrise. I buried her remains, and her unborn child. I did not even begin to pursue the monster for several hours. The scent had grown cold and the beast had put a great distance between us."

"I began my search, and for the next three months I tracked it, into what is now northern Europe. I lost myself to the hunt. I thought of nothing else. It moved ever north, always one step ahead of me. I often lost the scent for days and weeks at a time when it neared civilization. Inevitably it would kill, and the hunt would resume."

"I continued to sustain myself on the blood of animals. Even then I did so without taking life. The blood of animals will sustain us, but it leaves us ever thirsty. It is not an easy existence, but I could no longer take life. I was not the same. Through me he was reborn, and through him I too was reborn. But I was angry David, so hurt and very angry. I did nothing but hunt, wait, and ponder the nature of the beast I tracked."

"If you believe there is a God, and I believe you do, then you must also believe there is an adversary, a devil, an evil incarnate. The darkness lured me away from him the night he was transformed. It also tried to persuade me to kill the Roman. If I had, it would have been the first of many. I would have forgotten my new life and returned to a life of misery. And when I refused, it took him. It used him to take physical form. It then killed Mary and her child. It knew David; it knew where to find her. It knew everything. It prevented the birth of the product of the first union of a male and female vampire. I believe that was the intention from the start."

"In the year I tracked it I had not caught so much as a glimpse of it. I had followed its tracks and smelled its scent. I had found the blood soaked bodies of those it had slain, but I had not seen so much as a hair from its pelt. I had followed it to the north cape of what is now Norway. Human settlements were rare in that part of the world at that time and it was late fall. The sun no longer rose and the aurora borealis filled the perpetual night sky."

"I had not seen a human in some time. The few tribes of reindeer hunters had migrated south to avoid the arctic winter. I wondered if it could survive without human flesh upon which to feed. That is, until I found a mutilated reindeer carcass. I did still wonder why it had vanished when we had passed near human settlements. I was beginning to doubt I would ever find it. I wondered if it were capable of taking some intangible form, and by doing so lock me into an eternal chase."

"The trail no longer ran cold and I dared to hope that I might be close. I could smell the scent of salt in the air as I neared the sea. We were well within the Arctic Circle and the air was bitterly cold. We can suffer the cold quite well, but we are not impervious to its effects. However, I was old enough to withstand the freezing temperatures even with bare feet. I began to see spots of blood in its' snowy prints and I wondered how well it tolerated the subzero nights."

"It had not halted its thunderous pace in days. I was growing anxious and I was beginning to tire. I knew this place. I had crossed this land before. Something had to happen. It would have to turn back, perhaps attempt to evade me. It had to know I hunted it. Why else would it be so driven to cover so much ground at such a pace? Perhaps it would run into the sea, denying my vengeance. I quickened my pace. The scent was stronger. I was closing in."

"The ground was covered in snow. The wind had calmed and its tracks remained in the soft fine white powder. Have you ever seen the northern lights David?" I had seen pictures but nothing more.

"They are beautiful. Rolling waves of blue, green, red, pink, all colors, and all bright and luminous. It is magical, other worldly. It seemed a fitting place to encounter my enemy."

"That night I recalled my years spent as Sekhmet, the lion goddess of long ago, the lady of slaughter. I roared as I charged toward the cliffs. At last I would have my revenge, I would kill the beast. I topped the last of the hills that separated me from the sheer cliffs of Nordkapp. I saw him there along the cliff line. I made straight for it, but I saw not a beast. I saw a man, a weary man. He held up his palm in gesture to pause. He stood bent at the waist, bracing himself with his other hand against his bent knees."

"Please," he said between his labored breaths. "Please wait," he managed to say again.

"Now upon him I could see that it was in fact the Roman. Where is it, I screamed? Where is the beast? Where is the darkness? I demanded.

"Here," he said. "I couldn't stop. Please help me! They're not dead, none of them. It's in them now. They are all like me. Oh God what have I done? Get it out of me!" he screamed.

"I understood immediately why it had disappeared near human settlements. It had allowed him to be human. It had allowed him to be near people. It had killed dozens of people and it had never occurred to me that, thirsty as I was, I had not been drawn to their blood. They were not dead at all; they were all Werewolves as well."

"In some sort of incubation period much like our own, the implications were terrible. If each one were capable of creating new werewolves, their population would explode exponentially. I feared the world would soon be peopled with Werewolves. I needed to go back. Retrace the path we had cut across Europe and find them, find them all quickly. I knew I could not do it alone, and yet, for all I knew I was the last of my kind. I knew I would have to change that. But first I had to deal with the creature at hand."

"I believed he was beyond help. I did not know if killing him would kill the darkness within him. He stood there naked and shivering before me. His feet were badly frost bitten and bloody. Emaciated and suffering, he would have died from exposure soon enough."

"Ppplease," he implored through chattering teeth.

"Show yourself, I demanded. He began to whimper and cry. But slowly his sobs became low chuckles and escalated into full-blown laughter. He stood to his full height and glared down at me."

"You are weak and pathetic. You are nothing. You will never be as he is. You don't deserve his favor. He was wrong to choose you pathetic creatures over his own. I will not have you bring forth the next pathetic race of monkeys. If I could send you back to the primordial soup from which you crawled I would, but I can't. I can, however, kill you," he said with disgust."

"It was not the Roman speaking to me. It was the darkness, perhaps the Devil himself."

"You are welcome to try, I told him. He began convulsing and twisting. His body snapping and popping like before. In seconds he became the beast. It lunged at me. I tried to move, but I was not fast enough. It knocked me to the icy ground. He tore at my neck, opening a great wound. The pink snow steamed with my blood. I was mortally wounded. I had been arrogant and underestimated the beast. I was younger, weaker in those days."

"The wound began to close quickly but I had lost too much blood to sustain a fight more than a few moments. I had been thirsty for months, living on what little I could feed upon, but massive blood loss signals an overwhelming thirst. I could not manage the thirst and fight the beast at the same time."

"I would have died, had it not been for Aina. Her battle cry cut through the icy night air as swiftly as did her spear. The weapon plunged deep into its heart. It let out a deafening howl. Before it had finished its cry she had pulled the spear free and plunged it into the beast a second time. With what strength remained inside me I gripped its jaws and ripped its head in two. The darkness fled its filthy carcass. Disappearing over the cliffs, I faintly heard its crass laughter echo across the barren landscape."

"I was not the last of my kind after all. She had been tracking us for some time, unsure of what she followed. The beast had neared a village she protected, killing a young hunter. She set off after it and shortly after spotted my tracks as well. She was unaware of what she truly was. She had taken on the life of a goddess, fiercely protecting the people she once belonged to. But I knew instantly she was one of my descendants."

"And I knew we were of the same ilk," Ann broke in.

"It was you?" I asked.

"Yes it was David." Ann replied. "I was absolutely shocked. I had no idea what was happening. I had never seen a creature like that and I hadn't seen another like myself since the night I was made. I didn't even know her name, and now another had come. I was terrified she would leave without letting me ask her a million questions, but I feared her as well."

"I had no idea what her intentions were." Ann continued. "My guard was up, that is until she spoke to me. I knew she was my own when I heard her voice. I laughed out loud. She was speaking in an unfamiliar dialect of my own tongue and I could only glean bits of what she said, but it was enough to know that she meant me no harm. I had lived alone in the cold for such a long time with no one to belong to. I was elated to know I wasn't alone in the world. I had already forgotten the weeks I had spent trailing that demon."

"When I was changed I couldn't keep from feeding and I was driven away from my loved ones. My own people had shunned me, but I had nowhere else to go. I lingered nearby, and yes, I did satisfy my thirst. But I died a little inside every time I took the life of another. I was miserable and I probably would have made the choice to die, had a solution not presented itself."

"Another faction made war on my people. They came in the middle of the night. I heard them coming long before anyone in the village woke up. I drove them back, killing many of them. I protected my people from their and our, enemies. I became their guardian. I brought peace and stability to them. I loved them at a distance. But I was still alone, until the night Sonja came into my life."

"She took me to her hiding place in the cliffs. I sat with her and told her all that I knew, much as I am doing now with you. I told her of the possibility of more werewolves having been created and roaming Britannia. I asked for her help and, together, we made our way south."

"The Roman was right. There were more, many more. Together we built an army, an army of vampires. We hunted them successfully for decades. We followed strict guidelines. We took no human life, and I forbade anyone to attempt to create a male."

"We followed his teachings closely. We protected his church, which flourished under our protection in Europe. We were strong in number. For more than a thousand years we hunted them. We had all but wiped the werewolves out of existence. Then the plague struck Europe. It killed not only men, women, and children, but animals as well. Our source of survival became scarce. Our resolve crumbled. Many of us fled to faraway lands. Others began feeding on humans while others destroyed themselves. It was a terrible, terrible time."

"Werewolves began reproducing like a bacterium. Their disease was spreading at an alarming rate. Each new beast seemed to have an innate directive to kill and procreate. They are monsters."

"As you know, the conversion for us is much more difficult. The person you are remains intact if you can withstand the strain of rebirth. For many, it is too much and the mind becomes unstable. We have to be cautious, take our time, and be very selective. In looking back, I believe, had we not been so hasty to build our numbers we would not have collapsed in Europe."

"Fortunately for us, the Black Death not only claimed humans and animals, but in the second year it began claiming werewolves as well. This slowed their spread dramatically, but it did not seem to afflict vampires. Had it not been so, we would have been decimated. Ann, myself, and a few others remained in Europe through the years of the plague. Sickness and death lingered close, even unto us. But together, with the help of the plague, we nearly purged the continent of them. Nearly, but not completely."

"Benito Maresca was the last werewolf around. The decision to allow him to live was another link in a long chain of errors I had committed. Maresca was a man of the cloth. The Church had changed much. It was organized and powerful. It restricted access to knowledge and strove to keep the masses underfoot. But at its core were the same principals Yeshua put forth and Maresca upheld those teachings."

"He had been bitten and infected by a werewolf, some four months prior to our discovering him. He managed to keep the beast at bay, refusing to allow it to manifest itself. He was a man of remarkable faith and strength. In fact we never would have found him had it not been for a moment when his resolve wavered. He transformed, terrifying clergymen, but harming no one."

"Tales of a wolf demon made for popular chatter and word spread quickly. Once the news reached our ears, we made our way to the town of Sorrento where the stories of the demon that had been sighted fleeing the monastery of St. Francis originated. It was not difficult to locate him. The second need we have of respiration; passing air over the olfactory nerves, led us to his door. We told him who and what we were and what our purpose for being there was. He was frightened at first, but that soon gave way to relief. He had been under the belief that he was being punished or somehow tested by God and felt his lapse in resolve demonstrated his unworthiness."

"I admired his strength and humility. I chose to spare him. I often regret that lapse in my own resolve, but perhaps killing him would have been the greater of two evils."

"Once again I shared our history. It was difficult to believe that more than thirteen hundred years had slipped by since I had begun my own journey as a follower of Christ. He particularly enjoyed the personal stories of Yeshua that I shared with him. The night of my failure and the rise of the darkness troubled him greatly, but nonetheless, he accepted every word as truth."

"What was I to do? How was I to leave him there with the power to create another wave of monsters? Benito offered an easy solution: He would come with us."

"He feared he would succumb to the evil inside him. And so we lived. Staying for as long as we could, wherever we could. We established several successful churches in Europe and silently influenced Christianity throughout the centuries. Benito continued to carry the weight of his cursed soul without failure. The beast remained chained within him, though the strain of it betrayed his youthful face through his weary eyes."

"The three of us lived in harmony for some time. We eventually made contact with those vampires who had not fled Europe or ended their lives during the plague, twenty-three of us in all. We no longer maintained the structured organization of years past, but we remained in loose contact. Most of the others accepted Benito and shared my need to help him. He shared our love of God and of mankind. So long as he lived I wanted to help him to control the darkness within him."

"I felt responsible. After all, it was I who through indulgence of my own self-pity brought this demonic creature into the world of mankind. I often wondered how long Benito might have to live with this burden. How long would he have to coexist with the beast inside him?"

"He had lived far beyond the expected life of man, but he was still subject to illness and disease. His body was not like ours. He hungered, fatigued, and thirsted like a mortal man, but he did not age as a man should age. There were times that he seemed old and haggard and times that he looked the vibrant young man he was. I wondered if his body reflected the struggle within himself."

"He would not sleep unwatched. That is how he had allowed it to emerge in the Sorrento. Nightmares had haunted him. He had managed to avoid sleep for seven days before he collapsed and the beast took hold of him.

Still, he managed to do no harm and flee into the forest. Nightmares still came nightly but he suffered through them. He believed that it helped him to know Ann and I were standing guard at his bedside. He said that he could endure the dreams so long as we held vigil."

"However, time and constant torment took its toll. I cannot define the moment it began to go wrong, but Benito's behavior changed. He became increasingly eccentric. At first I suppose I ignored the signs, but you must understand that I had come to love him. You cannot share a life spanning centuries with another without developing a deep emotional bond. We all loved him. He became a great concern to everyone."

"He slowly began to withdraw from us. He spent more and more time alone. Keeping watch over him became a strain on both Ann and I. We summoned several of the others to join us in our efforts. Benito took this move as an act of aggression and withdrew even further. We were afraid we would push him completely away so we chose to back away from him. When we did he left us all together and took refuge in shrouded ranks of The Holy See, the governing body of the Vatican. We tried to contact him but he refused to see us. He knew we would not violate the sanctity of any church."

"The fear of not knowing what was happening to him began to consume me day and night. As I said, I had grown to love him and I believed he loved us as well. I wanted to help him but it seemed impossible. His unwillingness to communicate with us filled me with dread. I did not have the conviction to kill him so many years ago, and I knew I could not do it now. What if he loosed the demon? What then? Which of us would hunt and kill the man we had all come to love so dearly?"

"I was not alone in my fears. We all felt the same turmoil. Months went by with no word and without incident. Then the letter came. I can still remember the feeling of despair I felt as I read his words. He blamed me. He held me solely responsible for his affliction. He called me a liar. He said that I never knew Christ and that I had blasphemed God. He condemned us all to Hell, Spawns of Lucifer he called us. He said the full power of the church stood behind him and that our kind would be driven from Europe."

"I could not understand how things could have changed so quickly, but then I suppose it was not quickly after all. It was centuries of slow change, little things here and there, and I had been blind to it all. The Benito we all loved had gone. He had become a zealot. I can see it so clearly looking back, but then that is the nature of error."

"I had to assume that Benito had shown them what he was capable of becoming. That would have been the only way he would have been able to convince the church that we even existed and rally them against us so quickly. He even warranted a letter bearing the seal of the Pope himself. Now imagine our problem: Were we to kill a man with whom we still felt a deep love and kinship? A man who also served and loved God, a Christian man who in all the time we knew him managed to restrain the Devil himself. There was never any indication in all the lifetimes we shared that he would ever lose that control, or that he would ever wish to harm his fellow man in any way."

"We were all very hurt and very angry but the choice was clear. It was no longer possible to live as we had before. We would have to trust that he would not betray his faith. We would leave Europe. Once again we scattered to the four winds, but this time we set out with a purpose. We had always lived in the shadows of the church, a band of silent supporters hiding in the wings. But now we found ourselves positioned against that which we had struggled to protect."

"The Catholic Church had become the most powerful organization on earth and it was now aware of our existence. We departed as undead missionaries in search of new members to bring into our legions. In years past we had scrambled to create vampires quickly to extinguish the werewolf threat. This time we did so with methodology and structure. We founded The Church of The Lost Shepherd. Over the next few years we brought new members into our lifestyle and the Church simultaneously. The slow conversion proved successful and we lost very few to madness and death. But terrible events were unfolding within Benito's new circle. A new Pope had taken the helm. Pope Alexander VI had won the Papal election by means of silver and gold, purchasing the majority of votes."

"Upon his election, a man by the name of Giovanni di Lorenzo de' Medici, who later became Pope himself, issued a terrible warning ~ *"Now we are in the power of a wolf, the most rapacious perhaps that this has ever seen. And if we do not flee, he will inevitably devour us all."*

"When I read those words I knew Benito had been compromised. The monster released by a power hungry Pope who would stop at nothing to control and dominate. I cannot be sure if Benito was to blame or if in some fragile state he was duped into revealing the nature of his affliction thereby transferring the darkness into the hands of a man with the desire to exercise his own evil will. But to blame or not, the monster was out and Benito vanished from existence. We heard no word from him or news of his whereabouts."

"Alexander, however, wasted no time. The eldest of his sons, Cesara, who was infamously fathered during the years Alexander served as Cardinal, was his first victim. Once infected, he became a weapon that Alexander used to slay cardinals who opposed him and anyone else who stood in his path. This was so that his father, the wolf in Pontiff's clothing, could replace them with his burgeoning werewolf coven. We feared this new werewolf threat would lead to an open war with the Catholic Church. The darkness was yet unleashed upon the masses, the reigns held tight by the tyrant Alexander, but it was only a matter of time before it spilled into the world of man once again."

"I alone returned to Italy in hopes of discerning the fate of Benito Maresca, and to determine the nature and severity of the threat Alexander posed. Much to my surprise I was granted an audience with Alexander. He was truly a vile man and the darkness within him seemed to emanate from every pore of his stinking flesh, but he was not an unreasonable man."

"Benito had been sequestered deep within the bowels of the church, hidden away like so many earthly treasures. Once in the seat of power, Alexander had become privy to all the Church's secrets. He understood that Benito held an awesome power within the recesses of his tortured soul. He had forced it from him, deprived him of food, drink, and sleep until Benito had not the strength to resist his demands. Not only did Benito give his own secrets, he yielded ours as well. He told Alexander everything there was to know of us, including our numbers. Alexander realized that vampire kind posed a threat to his existence, and being no fool, he was unwilling to engage in a battle he felt he might possibly lose."

"It was an extremely tense bargaining session in which we were engaged. Unlike Benito, Alexander seemed to have no difficulty calling forth the beast and slipping back into human form again. Several times when tensions rose between us he shifted into the beast but I held my ground and showed no fear. I could not, however, hide my surprise at the ease with which he transformed. He said it was because Benito was weak and that he was a strong man. I believe it was because Benito was a good man and the darkness was unsettled in his body. Alexander was already a monster and evil was quite at ease within him."

"Our parley was fraught with difficulties, but in the end a treaty was struck between he and I. The werewolf population would increase no further and our numbers would hold fast as well. The Vatican would continue to hold Benito under their protection and five of our kind would be stationed within the Vatican City. We both agreed that it was in the best interest of all involved that both our species remain hidden from humanity. No human life was to be lost at the hands of either faction. The current treaty was to remain in effect so long as we both lived. Alexander would govern his own until his death at which time a new agreement was to be forged. Any violation of the agreement was to be punishable by death."

"Ann selected the five who would stand vigil within the Vatican. They would watch Alexander closely and report his movements and conduct to me. The killings did stop and he created no more werewolves. His opposition continued to grow in spite of his new restraint. And at the age of seventy-four his life was taken, poisoned by those closest to him. After a single day his body was so decomposed and rotten that the church of St. Peter's Basilica refused to accept it until forced to by Vatican mandate."

"I feared the horrific condition of his corpse would arouse suspicion as to his true nature, but to my relief it was accepted as common knowledge that he was poisoned and the state of his body was attributed to the effects of the agent he had ingested. It would seem we had a new friend, the enemy of our enemy, someone close to the Pope, aware or unaware of the devil within him, and had taken action from within the Church. With his abrupt demise I anticipated an upheaval within the disguised werewolf ranks of the Church, but instead they disappeared without a sound. Without so much as a whimper."

"They remained silent, invisible to the world and to us. In fact, they almost faded into legend save for those who hunted them in the days of old. It has become difficult for me to reckon time, David. So much has happened, so much

66

time has passed, and yet it seems no more than the blink of an eye. Years, decades, and centuries disappear like half uttered whispers."

"At the beginning of the new millennium there were three hundred and forty seven of us in all. We had lived unfettered and unnoticed for five hundred years. The world had changed and we had changed with it. In this new world science laid waste to mystery at an exponential rate, while the world of religion struggled to clutch them ever tighter like sand escaping a bony fist. We chose to embrace science. We had begun to examine the mystery of our kind, to unravel the secrets of what makes us what we are, as I understand Ann has already begun to explain this to you."

"Our church changed as well. We became no longer a church of vampires alone. Humans joined our church in droves, some of which are aware of our existence and others who simply believe in our message. With the identification of our variant Mitochondria and the duel aberrant strain, which you carry, came new hope of bringing forth the next male. I began to search for him, to search for you David, but I had been foolish to think the enemy had simply disappeared."

"We moved about the world boldly and freely, but all the while they were watching us. For all our senses, for all our marvelous gifts, we had not the slightest inkling we were under surveillance until the attacks began."

"Antoinette was the first. She had been with us since 1917. She was young, kind, humble, a beautiful creature both inside and out. She was killed in the summer of 2003. Her sweet, precious body mutilated by fang and claw. Her murder marked the beginning of the resurgence of werewolves."

"Many killings followed. They were swift and horrific, each one worse than the one before. They knew where to find us, when and where to strike. Our flock was quickly decimated. Oh David if only you could see things through my eyes for a moment. Her death and the death of so many others, all of the mistakes were mine. I am responsible for all of them."

"I am to blame, Benito was right. It all rests with me, and now the world is full of them David. They are everywhere. There are too many to fight, too many to overcome. With another severe miscalculation, another error in judgment, we have nearly diminished to oblivion. We are but nine, nine sheep in a world of wolves, awaiting our shepherd. And now you have come to us, my beautiful David."

Chapter Five

The Lord is my shepherd; I shall not want.
Psalm 23

A long uncomfortable silence filled the room. The lost Shepherd, the search for another male, not another since Christ, the implications of her tale were hitting home like a hammer.

"What do you want from me?!" I demanded.

"David, please accept your fate, you have been chosen by God," she replied.

"I'm not chosen by God or anyone else. I can't be what you need me to be. I can't be what anyone needs me to be. I am what I am, nothing more. I don't even talk to God. I don't want to talk to God. I don't want to be a part of this, I don't want to be a part of your church or anyone else's church or religion or cult or whatever the hell you have going on here. I'm alone. I like being alone. I don't need this crap! I'm out of here!"

I ran from the room, down the hall and through the doors leading into the main chapel. To my shock, the pews were full of wide-eyed men, women, and children. All eyes

69

were fixed on me. I froze in my tracks like an animal caught in headlights.

Alexander and a younger child with shaggy blonde hair sprang from a nearby pew and hurried to my position in the rear of the cavernous chapel.

"Mr. Cross, sir. Please don't move like that in here," he whispered from directly in front of me.

"Humans can't see you when you move that fast. You have to be careful in the presence of people." The other, smaller child added.

"Come with us please, Sir." Alex said as firmly as he could with his trembling voice.

I wasn't sure if it was nervousness or adolescences wavering in his words but I found it endearing which ever it was. The other boy was shorter and stockier than Alexander and he looked to be about ten years old but he exuded the confidence of a much older child.

"Trust us." the younger child whispered.

"People keep saying that to me around here, "I whispered back.

"Then maybe you should start," he whispered with a grin.

The two of them were very disarming and I felt compelled to allow them to rescue me from the situation. They led me down a long hall in the center of the back of the building to a small clerk's office. There were several laptops and a few filing cabinets, a few chairs and two small wooden desks. We filed inside the room and Alexander closed the door.

"That was awesome!" The younger of the two shouted once the door latched shut.

"Luke! Be quiet!" Alexander cautioned. "You can't just appear like that in front of people, they're not ready." Alexander scolded, obviously embarrassing himself in the process.

"Shut up Alex, the door hitting the wall scared everyone. It was just loud. Nobody saw anything". Luke countered.

"You shut up!" Alex said slugging Luke on the shoulder.

"Why aren't you two afraid me, of vampires? I mean, well, what do you two know?" I stammered.

"What do you mean?" Luke asked.

"I mean do you know what I am?" I asked.

"Well of course we do, do you know what you are?" Luke asked.

"No, no not really, I don't think I do, "I replied.

"I think you're scared." Alex said while trying to bolster his wavering voice.

"No he isn't!" Luke countered. "Besides they won't come here," he continued.

"Who won't come here?" I asked.

"Those hairy freaks, they won't mess with you as long as you're here or any church. They won't fight in church. You're safe here." Luke assured me.

"So you know about them?" I asked.

"Yes" they both answered sharing a glance.

"Were you leaving?" asked Alexander.

"I was but I don't know where to go" I replied.

"If you leave by yourself they'll kill you." Alex said.

"What about you? What about all those people in there?" I asked.

"It's Tuesday night service." Alexander said flatly "They're supposed to be here," he continued.

"What happens when they leave?" I asked.

"They don't take human life if that's what you are asking. They don't like us. They think we worship vampires. But they leave us alone; sometimes they even try to convert those of us who know." Alexander said.

"Yeah and I heard some people were killed once in the New Zealand mission." Luke chimed in. "But I don't know if that's true or not. Ann says it probably wasn't werewolves but they all went there to check things out. They don't tell us much," he continued.

"And for good reason" Ann said opening the door. "Go to class, both of you. Joshua is waiting." Both boys exited quickly without a word.

"Whose kids are they?"

"They are mine."

"I don't understand"

"They're adopted. I have adopted many, many children over the years. It brings me joy. I love children. I brought them all up in the church. They know nothing but love for God and their fellow man. I don't pretend to be their mother but I love them all with all my heart. They know what I am, what we are. They don't know of life any other way. You have met Alexander and Luke. Joshua is nineteen, he teaches the children's class. Sean is twenty-one; he's still in New Zealand. He is due to come home Saturday."

"What happened in New Zealand?"

"There's a small church in the Southern Alps, only a handful of members and one of us. It was a very small branch. We had planned to close it down. It was too dangerous, too isolated but Mia had been there far too long to walk away. Six weeks ago they were all killed. The church caught fire with everyone inside. Their bodies were found crowded at the doors, as if they'd been barred shut. Mia would have been strong enough to tear the doors from the hinges but from appearances she simply huddled at the door with the others."

"There was an official investigation and a fair amount of media coverage. The investigation determined they'd died of carbon monoxide poisoning. Mia couldn't have though. She must have burned to death. She huddled with them at the doors and allowed herself to burn to death. Why they didn't escape is a mystery. She could have broken the stone itself if she had wanted to. The wooden doors should not have prevented their escape. We combed every inch of the area but we found no evidence of werewolf involvement. We returned with questions unanswered while Sean remained behind to settle with the insurance company and to see to the details of the property.

They might not have been involved but they are killing us David. We won't survive the decade. Please don't go. Please don't leave us. We need you." Pools of ochre red tears gathered in the corners of her eyes. A single blink sent them cascading down her flawless cheeks. She seemed so vulnerable, tender and yet I knew her sleek frame housed an un-gauged strength. The contrast between her outer strength and her inner sadness added to the depth of her beauty. I was denying it even at that moment but I had fallen in love with her. I knew I couldn't leave. I had no one and nowhere to go and even if I'd had another option I wouldn't have taken it. I was bound to her and didn't realize it but only because the bonds that tied us had not been tested.

I stayed at the church without leaving the grounds for the next few days. Ann and I spent every possible moment together. With her help I made peace with what I had become physically and I began to enjoy the way my new vampire body performed. As Luke so plainly stated, it's awesome.

The children came and went often. I hadn't seen anything except the walls of the church but Ann's home was nearby. The older child Joshua expertly served as steward to the other boys in the time Ann spent with me. We talked to each other constantly. I hadn't let down my guard to enjoy the company of another since Sarah went away. It was nice. But by Friday evening the mood had changed. I felt something was about to happen, like the calm before a storm. Later that night I was in the cottage with Ann, it was almost midnight when Sonja came in.

"It is time, child," she said to Ann in her distinct unfamiliar accent.

"Let's go David." Ann said.

I didn't know where we were going, but as soon as I walked into the chapel I knew what was happening. The other seven had gathered. I'm generally shy, uncomfortable being noticed. I like to fade into the background. The lights in the large room were dim but there was no fading into the background. I could see the expressions on their faces clearly enough to discern their thoughts, but I think I would have known their thoughts even in the dark. I felt them. The room was charged with their presence. I sensed fear, wonderment, awe, elation and it was all directed at me.

Ann again took my hand to comfort me. "It's alright David," she whispered. She led me up the center isle with Sonja close behind. We sat in a row of gilded chairs behind the pulpit where Sonja stood. The seven sat scattered among the first two rows. Each face, each set of eyes fixed on me until Sonja broke the silence.

"My daughters, I know you have placed yourselves at great risk by traveling here on such short notice. But much has happened and I wanted you all to be here to hear what I have to say. Tears of blood were already streaming down most of their faces. I sensed they were all trying to contain an impending explosion of emotion. With a slight tremble in her own voice, Sonja spoke the words "The Shepherd has returned." The room spun and went black.

***

"David." The old man spoke softly. He sat next to me on the bank of a fast moving river. I sat up and I filled my chest with the cool damp air. It felt good. "You chose to come, David. The river has already swollen, and rain is coming."

***

When I awoke I was back in the small parsonage. Ann, Sonja and Joshua were with me.

"Are you alright?" Ann asked.

"I think so, I don't know what happened, "I said.

"You fainted," she informed me.

"Men don't faint, mother. They pass out." Joshua broke in.

"Thanks" I said. "I'm okay. It was like they were inside my head. I felt their emotions. Are they gone?" I asked.

"No, they are still here," Sonja answered. "They are waiting to speak with you," she continued.

"I am not what you think I am Sonja, I'm just a man. I'm no leader, I'm no savior."

"God calls who he will. It is your choice to answer, David."

I didn't tell her about the dreams. I didn't see the need. I didn't know for sure what they meant or if they meant anything at all, but I felt something in them. Maybe He was talking to me. I just didn't understand why He would bother. I had turned my back on him. I didn't have faith in anything but myself. But I was tired of resisting. And her words rang true. "What do I need to do?"

"They simply wish to know you as I do. Speak with them. Then we must hold counsel. A course of action must be decided."

"What do you mean?"

"Sean is missing." Ann Answered. He failed to report in and we can't reach him by phone. He was supposed to check in and given the circumstances we are assuming the worst."

"I'm ready, "I said. The four of us re-entered the main structure but the chapel was now empty. There was a narrow banister to the right of the pulpit. They lead me down it to a stone walled room beneath the chapel. A long wooden table with ten chairs split the small room in two. The seven other matriarchs sat waiting and watching. Ann and Sonja each took a seat at the far end of the table. I sat in the remaining empty seat at the head of the table. Again all eyes were fixed on me. I broke the silence which I am sure didn't last as long as it seemed.

"I'm David, "I said. Smiles and soft laughter followed. The vampire to my left had a regal presence, her posture was impossibly perfect and her jet-black hair caught the flickering light of the candles around the room.

"I am Glenda," she said with a warm smile as she lightly touched my hand, I was relieved by her open warmth. I imagined she would have been about the age my mother should have been. But her actual age was impossible to determine.

They went around the room introducing themselves in turn. "Lorelei", "Oksana", "Rosa", "Bacia", "Mieko", "Katherine". They were all so different from one another but all possessed the same surreal beauty. Each shared her own unique story with me. With each one I gained a deeper understanding of their faith in God and their love of mankind. I could not imagine these beautiful creatures were ever the monsters of legend. Instead I saw them as something more, something wondrous. They were creatures with the potential to change the course of mankind.

I had some deep sense that I was on the right road. It had to be part of Gods plan. I accepted my fate. I would be whatever they needed me to be. It's strange but in the hours that followed, as I looked around that table, I grew to close those women. I began to feel like I had always known them.

And then there was Ann, every time our eyes met it was like we were sharing something. A thought or a moment, there was something there, some kind of connection, an understanding. I knew she was worried about Sean but I sensed there was something more. I was almost certain it was pain she was feeling. After a time the focus shifted from me to the situation with Sean. They all agreed that some unforeseen event had prevented Sean from contacting Ann at the designated time. But all, save Ann, felt it wise to wait for him to return. Ann strongly disagreed with the decision but apparently Sean had been cause for much undue distress in the past and it was assumed that this situation was no different.

I learned there were other children as well, a lot of other children. Each Vampire had her own adoptive family, some, more than others but they all had sons, and all were members of the church and all were fully aware of what their guardians were.

I managed to put it together that Sean had exposed the family to risk several times, and that he had been the only problem child. Their opinions and feelings seemed to vary. Rosa expressed disapproval with the decision to allow him to see to the final details in New Zealand while Katherine supported Ann's efforts to guide him back into the fold.

"There isn't any other way but to love him and trust him." Katherine said with a smile that lit up her face and the entire room. Her eyes were a startling shade of blue and her whole affect was one of tenderness and warmth. There was no other way but to love these women.

Ann was distraught. I could sense it. I wanted to be alone with her. I wanted to talk to her about Sean. I wanted to know what she was thinking. Right on cue she excused herself from the table. I was about to excuse myself as well but I hesitated for a moment as I wondered if it would seem rude to leave their company.

But before I could speak, Glenda again touched my hand gently. "Go to her David, she needs you."

"Don't you worry about us. We all have a lot to talk about. You go talk to her." Katherine reiterated. I detected a hint of a southern accent in her delightful voice. Each of the others gave their nod of approval.

I mounted the stairs moments behind her but she was already in the parsonage by the time I reached the top of the stairs. In the absence of human eyes I explored the boundaries of my vampire body and covered the distance to the parsonage doors as fast as I could manage. I stopped just outside the doors but the air before was compressed so quickly that it blew the doors open with unexpected force.

"You could have just knocked, David."

"Sorry, I wasn't expecting that to happen."

"It's alright, you'll get used to the physics of being a vampire in a few hundred years."

"I'm going, David. I'm going to find Sean. I have a terrible feeling that something has happened to him."

"The others, they don't seem too surprised, "I replied.

"David, I know him. Yes he has been in trouble a great deal in the past. He has caused me more than his fair share of heartache but he knows how serious things have become. New Zealand has affected him. He wanted to take care of things there. He wanted the responsibility. He's back on the path David. He would not have frightened me like this now. I know it." Watery drops of blood spilled to the floor as she spoke.

"Ok, so what do we do?"

"I'm going alone David."

"I'm not letting you go without me, Ann."

"David, we can't risk losing you."

"What are you planning to do? Keep me in here forever?"

"No, I suppose not, but we need you to stay safe until…"

"Until what, Ann?"

"Until we can find a way to keep you safe."

"I know what's going on Ann; I know what it is you want."

"What is it I want, David?"

"A child."

"You believed her didn't you?"

"Don't you?"

"Yes," she replied. "But it isn't what I want; it's what we all want. It's what we need. We are being exterminated, David. You may be the last chance we have to save ourselves."

"And who is to be the other half of this Adam and Eve relationship?"

"I'm afraid your choices are a bit limited."

"Is it my choice?"

"It is, but I had hoped to influence your decision."

"I don't know, I think Meiko may have intentions of her own. Are you sure you want to leave me here?"

"Okay, you're coming with me but we have to go now. Alexander is making the preparations."

"What will the others say?"

"We aren't telling them, we're just going," she replied.

We hurried out of the building at a vampire pace. Alexander had the car out front running and waiting. It felt like I'd been released from indenture stepping outside the church grounds.

"Is the Plane ready, Alexander?" he was breathing heavily from carrying out the hasty preparations.

"Yes Miss Falen, everything is ready," he said as he loaded bags into the trunk. "Miss Falen... Mother, please be careful. I don't want to lose you too."

"I promise I will come back... I promise Alex," she said as she embraced the young man.

"They're out there; I can feel it, Mother. I saw a blacked out van driving by slow today. I don't feel safe here anymore."

"Go back inside, stay with the others. They will keep you safe. Go, hurry," she kissed him on the forehead and sent him running back to the church.

We climbed into the car, she revved the engine, slammed it in gear and we were off. It was a little un-nerving to be flying down darkened streets again, Ann was staring into the rear view mirror more than she was looking at the road ahead. I glanced over my shoulder frequently but I felt compelled to watch the road for her. There was no pursuit. We reached the airport and boarded the plane without difficulty. The long range Gulf Stream easily traversed the distance from Rhode Island to Los Angles. But we had to land at LAX to refuel before completing the final leg of the journey. I could tell that Ann was far less comfortable on the ground.

"We're not safe anywhere, are we Ann?"

"No, we're not."

"What about the pilots, do you trust them?"

"Yes, they are members of the church, and we pay them handsomely."

"If you don't mind my asking, how do you pay for all of this?"

"I don't mind at all, when you know you are going to live for hundreds, maybe thousands of years, long term investments aren't a problem," she replied as she peered intensely out the window. Suddenly she called out to the pilot.

"Get us out of here, quickly!"

"Yes ma'am, "I heard the voice on the other end respond.

"Ann, what's wrong?"

"We've been on the ground too long. I don't like it. Something doesn't feel right," she picked up the phone and spoke to the pilot again

"Get us out of here now!"

"Ma'am we haven't been cleared for takeoff.

"Get this plane off the ground or I will!" she roared.

My apprehension was mounting by the second, "What's happening Ann? What do you see out there?" I asked, as she glared through one of the many oval windows.

She pointed to two men in jump suits moving toward the plane. "There." They looked like airport personnel to me.

"Werewolves!" she growled.

"How do you know!?"

Without answering she stormed the cockpit. The pilot and co-pilot turned in their seats with alarm when she burst through the door.

"Move the freaking plane now!" The co-pilot radioed the tower requesting take-off again. We were cleared just as Ann's hand assisted the pilot's push of the hefty yolk. The massive engines responded instantly and we surged toward the runway. The two men who had been walking toward us were sprinting back toward the hanger as Ann came back and joined me at the window.

"How did you know?" I asked.

"There was no reason for them to be there. And the way they move, it's with purpose. They all move with such purpose. It gives me chills. I'll never forget the way they move. I have to call Sonja," she quickly dialed the number on her cell phone. "Sonja, were at LAX. They know we're here. There were two of them. I don't know. That's twice we've escaped them. No, I only saw the pair. No they didn't. I don't know Sonja. It doesn't make sense. I know. You know I had to come. I will. I will call as soon as I know something," she ended the call and turned to me.

"David, I know it was a difficult night and your mind was not your own but after you were made and you encountered the werewolf, you said it attacked you. Think back. Did it attack you; I mean was it trying to kill you?" she asked.

"I don't know, I sure thought so. I mean it scared the hell out of me. But maybe it's possible that it wasn't. I just remember feeling afraid for my life, I got angry, I wanted to kill it. I had my hands around its throat and... And maybe I attacked it; maybe it was fighting for its life. I don't know Ann. I don't know. Why, what did she say?" I asked.

"I don't know David, something just isn't right. The night you came to me, it was too easy to get away. And just now, David I'm not sure they want to kill you at all. I need to think," she eased into one of the plush recliners and into deep thought. The soft dinging of the fasten seat belt notification as we turned onto the runway brought her back to the moment. "Not one of us has survived their attacks since they resurfaced. They know everything about us and we know nothing about them. But I am beginning to think that they don't want to kill you at all. I think they want you to live."

We began our take off and the welling thirst coupled with the sudden acceleration left me with a sick emptiness. Once we were air-born again and our speed leveled out the vague hollow feeling subsided but the thirst did not.

"Ann, I need to drink."

"I'm sorry David, Of course. I don't mean to be insensitive. Don't worry; there are provisions on this flight," she produced the familiar metallic cylinder from a small kitchenette in the rear of the cabin. I loved the warm rush the blood sent through my mind and body. Each time I drank the life giving fluid, I felt more alive than I had ever felt in my prior life.

Ann did not require the frequent nourishment that I required. She seldom fed and when she did, she consumed very little. I however drank like an addict getting his fix. I had never fed alone. I had always been with Ann. Each time she had to caution me to stop. I wasn't sure I would have otherwise. Several times I had consumed more than I should have and it resulted in a giddy drunkenness, which Ann thoroughly enjoyed. This time was no exception.

"David," She cautioned. "Slow down."

"I was just about to stop, I'm learning my limits, "I said with a quick wink. I loved to wink at her. It always brought a smile.

"I suppose you may as well indulge a little. It's a long flight to Auckland. I'll join you," she said as she produced two more canisters from the kitchenette.

"Will they follow us?" I asked as she handed me the cylinder of life giving blood.

"I don't know, we were planning to fly into Christchurch airport but after leaving LA we've changed our flight plan. If they did know where we were going, I hope the change of itinerary will buy us some time."

The world outside the aircraft was cold and black but inside the softly lit interior, I was basking in the warmth of the intoxicating fluid spreading through my body. I closed my eyes and sprawled across the generous couch. It began with the slightest touch of her delicate fingers caressing my face. A whispery kiss brushed my lips. I wanted her. In my heightened state, I needed her.

I didn't want to move. I feared if I opened my eyes that the desire would dissipate like a thin mist. But the next kiss solidified the moment. It was hard and deep. She bit my lip and my own warm blood mingled with our lips I could be still no more. I wrapped my arms around her and pulled her against me with immortal strength. She responded by ripping my arms free and forcing them to the couch above my head. She was stronger than I had imagined, maybe stronger than I was. Her grip was like steal; she held my arms tight as she explored another deep kiss. I bit her bottom lip as she kissed me. The taste of her blood was maddening. I was lost to all reason, all thought. I was an animal, nothing more. She released my arms and I tore at her clothes as she ripped my shirt from my chest. Our union was like no other experience on earth or above. I could never put into words the feelings of primal pleasure I felt. I loved her strength, her beauty and her passion. I wanted to consume her and to be consumed.

The hours passed as we embraced in still silence. It was strange to be that close to another and not hear the sounds of rhythmic breathing or feel the beating of a heart. We were motionless, statues bound in one another's unyielding embrace. As I held her I realized that all of the walls I had built to isolate myself had crumbled at the hands of the creature I held in my arms. I wondered if I could trust my feelings, were they my own?

It had been less than two weeks since I had awakened in a new world, as a new being. Each new interaction, each new experience, no matter how mundane became a journey of new discovery. The transformation itself, the fight with the werewolf, Sonja's story, the dreams, and feelings I had already been having for Ann. And now this, all of it together was almost more than I could get my mind around. I held a goddess in my arms, a mythical creature come to life. But I was no longer a mortal man. I had become as she. I too had reached forth my hand and taken of the tree of life.

***

"It's beautiful isn't David." The old man asked as he gently cupped a tiny, brilliant blue frog. We were standing in an immense forest. Thin beams of sunlight shattered in the dense canopy of trees above. "Beautiful but deadly," he continued. "Does that make it evil David? If this tiny little thing killed ten men, would it be an evil thing?" he asked.

"I suppose it would be to the ten men, "I answered.

"Yes, evil to whom?" he smiled warmly.

***

"You were dreaming again, weren't you?"

"Yes"

"What was the dream about?"

"Does it bother you that I dream?"

"I don't understand it, David. I wonder why you dream, and I don't. Do you think we were cursed by God in the beginning?"

"I don't know. I believe Sonja has lived a very long time. I believe that myth and legend come from some distant truth. I also know that I have said some very cruel things to God. I turned my back to Him; shut Him and everyone else out of my life. But I don't believe he would ever curse me for it. I believe He loved me even when I didn't love Him."

"I have devoted my life to God and to the betterment of mankind. I have served him faithfully but he does not let me dream."

"I don't understand it either Ann, but I feel very strongly that he is talking to me. How long was I asleep anyway?"

"A couple hours. David, you still breathe in your sleep, and you snore!" She proclaimed with laughter. I spent the rest of the flight pondering my dreams and trying to sort out my feelings for Ann.

***

It was winter in New Zealand. The cool sea air blasted my exposed skin. Again I was preoccupied by the new experience. I felt the cold air on my face and arms but I didn't experience the feeling of being cold. It, like so many other firsts, was mesmerizing. Ann prodded me down the stairs to the tarmac where a black Range Rover sat running and waiting for us.

"Don't we have to go through security?"

"Money expedites a great many things, David."

We climbed inside the SUV and were again greeted with the familiar, "Welcome back Miss Falen." Our driver was a young man with hard lines across his brow, sun-bleached, white hair and a blinding smile. He was dressed in the same manner Ann's children had been dressed.

"I wish I could bring her back Samuel," she said with obvious sadness as she put her hand on the boys shoulder.

"Ta ma'am, I know ya would. I miss her heaps but she ain't comin' back. Let's just find ya boy and maybe find out what happened to her too," he answered. She smiled a knowing smile and touched his golden face. "Now we'd better get A into G if we're gonna get to Waikikamukau before sun up tomorrow," he said in his thick down-under accent.

"What did he say?" I asked Ann.

"He said we'd better get going if we are going to get to Lake Tekapo by tomorrow morning," she said with a wink to Samuel.

"Why kick a moo cow?" I asked with concern.

"You know BFE, the middle a nowhere," Samuel answered. "Is this him? Is he the one we've been waitin' for all these years?" Samuel asked.

"He is. Samuel, this is David Cross."

"Pleased to make your acquaintance, I wish me mum coulda laid eyes on ya. Woulda meant the world but let's get the heck outta here." Be it through his eyes, his words or the touch of his skin when he shook my hand, I experienced a moment of the pain and loss he felt. He let go my hand, gave a saddened smile and turned back around in his seat. Gently put the car in to drive and then stomped the accelerator to the floor.

I was certain that Auckland was the most beautiful city on earth, even at night. But as the sun rose on the land of the long white cloud the magnitude if its beauty overcame me. Until that day I hadn't seen anything more beautiful than East Tennessee but God lingered a little longer when he created New Zealand. It will forever be for me, the place by which all others are gauged.

We rode in silence as Samuel drove expediently down the West Coast of the north island. Ann and I, both lost in thought, sat gazing out the windows. So much in my life had changed so quickly that I still struggled to make sense of it all. It was easy to get lost in my own mind in those days. My thoughts inherently went back to the beginning. I was trying to remember the entire day of the accident. I had a nagging feeling there was something important I needed to remember but it was all so hazy. The train of thought inevitably ended where I sat and with many more questions.

"Mia was your mother?" I asked, ending the easy silence.

"She was. I'm part Maori, part Kiwi, kind of a misfit if ya know what I mean. Ended up in an orphanage when I was a pup. Mia adopted me on sight, paid cash outright. Took me home, raised me as her own. I loved her."

"I'm sorry."

"Me too, mate, me too," he replied. "I shoulda been there."

"It was not your fault Sam." Ann said.

"Maybe, maybe not. Just the same, I shoulda listened to her more. Ya know me and your boy have a lot in common," he said as he glanced at Ann in the rear view mirror.

"It's not always an easy life Sam."

"No, reckon it's not for sure. I had my share a problems. Knowin' the world ain't what it seems, Knowin' she was gonna live on long after I shriveled up and died. Guess I was wrong on that count, wasn't I? My life coulda been a lot worse. I had everything I needed and most of what I wanted. The way I see it, she saved me and I let her down. I wanna find out what happened and I never believed those filthy devil dogs didn't kill'em. And I tell ya what, neither does Sean."

"What do you mean, what did he say?"

"He spent a lot a time up there, said he found something, something terrible but wouldn't tell me what. Started actin' all dodgy. Started askin' me all sorts of questions about Sonja and mum. Wanted to know why I thought Sonja wanted to close the church, wanted to know if I knew the reason they didn't see eye to eye. Truth is I didn't know much. I'd been so wrapped up in me own life I didn't know what was happenin' in the church or with mum."

"I got a call from her a couple a weeks before the fire. Said she just called to tell me she loved me. Sounded sorta sad. Didn't think much of it at the time. Thought she was just disappointed in me. I had a few beers in me and I thought she could hear it in me voice. But now I think there was something goin' on, especially now. Ma'am I dunno what ya boy found out up there but it had something to do with whatever happened that night, mark my words."

"Strange things are happening Sam. I don't know what to make of it all. I don't even know if he's alive. I don't know where to start looking." Ann said.

"I didn't want to say nothing on the tele but he said for me not to look for him if anything happened. Said you'd come looking and to give you this," he handed her a sealed envelope keeping one hand and both eyes on the road. She opened it slowly and carefully as if she was afraid to disturb the contents. Inside she found a thin chain with a simple silver cross and a note with the words *Trust no one. Meet me in the lost gone at sunset.*

"What does it say?" I asked. She read the note aloud and placed the necklace around her neck.

"I know this land from the North Cape to the Bluff and I ain't never heard of no lost gone," Sam said with a quick curious look on his face.

"It's a place from his childhood. It's where he used to hide when he was frightened. But why would he let me come all the way here, only to go back home to find him?" she asked.

"I'm telling ya, he was actin' all cloak and dagga maybe it's a clue or a hint or somethin'," Sam replied.

"Where was the lost gone?" I asked.

"Sean was six when I found him. I knew he was too old to make the adjustment into our world but he was so sad and lonely. I couldn't leave him. His eyes called to me. So I took him home against all advice. He had a sense about him. He saw the world around him through a much older child's eyes.

The day I brought him home Joshua scaled a tree in the back yard. He fell from a high branch. I was in the kitchen with Sean when I heard Josh scream. I caught him just before he hit the ground; my movements terrified Sean. He ran from the house. I followed him but I let him go. I didn't want to frighten him any further. He ran to a cemetery down the street and huddled against one of the head stones. He fell asleep there. It made him feel safe. His mother had died only a few months earlier. He felt close to her in the cemetery. Whenever he was scared, sad or angry I knew I could find him there. He called it the lost gone."

"What was the name of the cemetery?" I asked.

"Pleasant Point," she replied.

"Aye ma'am there's a town called Pleasant Point on the way to Lake Tepako. It's not too far off the beaten path. There's a bone yard there and, it's called the Pleasant Point cemetery," he said with excitement.

"Sam listen, they know everything about us. Maybe we lost them after LA, I don't know, but they may have been watching you too. Can you get us there before sunset and without being seen?" she asked.

"You bet I can," he answered with a smile. We took the Wellington ferry to Picton on the South Island. From there we abandoned paved roads. Samuel subjected the Range Rover to the roughest roads the South Land had to offer. Some of them weren't even roads; they were no more than washed out goat trails. Cross-country routes added hours to an already long drive but young Samuel insisted he needed no rest.

We had traveled all day only stopping for fuel and Sam's human needs. Ann had packed a number of small flasks of nourishment for ourselves, which we used sparingly. It was nearing dark when we rolled out of a field onto the streets of Pleasant Point. Ann felt confident that we hadn't been followed and doubly so that if this were the place he'd be that no one would know but the three of us. We eased down Main Street and slowed in front of Nelligan's Hotel, Ann looking for any sign of Sean as we passed.

"It's just up ahead. There on the left," Sam said. The narrow unpaved road into the cemetery was heavily wooded and the setting sun barely penetrated the thick wall of foliage. The Rovers headlights came on in response to the darkened road. I sensed Ann's anxiety mounting as we entered the clearing that held the small, deserted graveyard.

"There's nobody about," Sam said peering through the windshield. "Maybe it's not the right place," he continued.

"No. This has to be the place," she answered as she opened the car door. The door had only opened a few inches when she suddenly froze, a look of alarm painted on her motionless face. A split second later I caught the same scent. It wasn't over powering at all. I might not have noticed at all if not for the expression on Ann's face. But it was there, a vague musky aroma.

"There!" shouted Sam. A lone figure stood motionless against the darkening backdrop of dense trees.

"Sean, what have you done?" she whispered to herself.

I could see clearly the figure was that of a young man. He began to walk slowly in our direction. I recognized the now familiar movements he made, an air of bold invulnerability and a distinctive swagger.

"Ann he's one of them!" I said to her. She didn't respond. She sat motionless as if trying to decide what she should do. I was just about to tell Sam to get us out of there when Sean halted his advance.

"I have to go to him," she whispered.

"I'm going with you, "I answered.

"Hold on now, I can't let the two of you just go waltzin' out there. Not if you're sayin' what I think you're sayin'," Sam added.

"I don't like this Ann, "I said.

"I'm going," she answered. She got out of the car before I could protest any further. I climbed out quickly to join her at the front of the car. Together we made our way toward the lone wolf.

Our bodies cast long shadows in the headlights as we navigated the tombstones on our way to the center of the graveyard. The faintly sweet scent I caught in the car became overpoweringly thick as we neared him, like the smell of a cheap cigar in a small room. Ann stopped a meter or so away from him. We were close enough to read the pained expression on his face.

"Please don't cry mom," he said.

"Sean, how could you have let this happen?" she asked choking back tears.

"Mom wait, it isn't like you think. Were you followed?" he asked.

"Were we followed? Is that all you have to say? Followed by whom, Sean?" she asked with a flash of anger in her voice. She continued without giving him a chance to respond. "Followed by your new pack? Is that what you mean?!" she demanded, tears streaming down her face.

"No mom, followed by the others," he answered.

"No Sean, we weren't followed. Why would they follow us?" she asked.

"Mom, It's Sonja. She killed them. She killed them all. She killed Mia," he said gravely.

"How dare you!" she scolded.

"It's true, mom. I can prove it," he said.

"No, No Sean. No you can't! It isn't true. They've poisoned your blood and your mind! They killed them.

They're monsters and Heaven help you, you're a monster now too."

His nostrils flared and his voice quaked as he spoke. "I'm not a monster. None of them are. You're in danger mom but not from any of them or from me. You have to listen to me," he pleaded.

Sam had grown tired of waiting in the car and joined us in the center of the cemetery. "What's goin' on mate?" he said to Sean.

"Help me talk to them Sam. Tell them about Mia's trouble with Sonja," he urged.

"All that's true enough but I wanna know what it was you said you found up there at church," Sam said. "Right!" he said with exuberance, obviously pleased to be out of the focus of his mother's fury for a moment. "This," he replied as he pulled a small tarnished key from his pocket. "It's to a safe deposit box in Wellington. It took some time to find it but I did. It was Mia's. She figured it out. She knew Sonja was responsible. I found lists, dates, locations; she had been tracking Sonja's activities," he said.

"Sean, I have known Sonja for nearly two thousand years. This isn't possible." Ann replied.

"It's all been about him, mom" He said as he nodded towards me.

"What do you mean?" I asked.

"Control, it's all about control, she has controlled us all. Everything has been a lie. Everything she said, everything she did has been about you, David. She knew you before you were born. Your mother, your father, your grandparents. She has manipulated everything. There have been no accidents.

Mia figured it out and persuaded Antoinette to do some investigating. Sonja found her snooping and she killed her. After that Mia had no doubts. She made contact with the werewolves. She went looking for the truth. Sonja killed her too, Mom. She killed all of the others. She's insane mom. She has to be stopped. I followed the trail Mia left behind. It led me to them, it led me to Benito," he said.

"Benito?!" she exclaimed. "He's alive?"

"Yes, he's here. And he wants so see you," Sean said. "Come with me. Trust me, please."

"Mate, am I gettin' this right? You're one of those dogs now?" Sam asked.

"He is Sam." Ann said.

"Bugger me!" Sam exclaimed. "How?!"

"I'll tell you everything if you'll just come with me. Mom please, I know you're hurt but you have to believe me," he pleaded.

"No, Sean. I can't. I won't believe this lie. They have poisoned you," she said choking back tears.

"David, please," he said. Ann hadn't told him my name but twice he had called me David.

"How do you know my name?" I asked.

"I know everything there is to know about you. I know it was no accident you ended up in that hospital," he said.

His words struck me like a roll of quarters to the back of the head. The thing I was trying to remember, that nagging feeling that I had forgotten something. It came roaring back into memory. I remembered checking my voicemail before leaving the house the morning of the accident. *"Don't go,* "It was a short, cryptic message from an unfamiliar number and the voice was barely more than a feminine whisper. I assumed it was a misdial and dismissed it but in the light of Sean's words it seemed like another piece to an expanding puzzle. The memory had been lost until that very moment.

"Ann, you said yourself that something's not right. Maybe he's telling the truth. I think someone tried to warn me not to go out that day. I think we should go with him, "I said.

"I'm with David. Wolf or no wolf, if Sonja had anythin' ta do with me mum's death, then I wanna find out what, I'm goin'," Sam said.

"He wants to see you again, Mom. He's here, waiting for you," Sean said. "I know how hard this is for you. I know I have put you through a lot, Mom. But you have to trust me. Sonja isn't what you think she is. She's dangerous. All of us are in danger. She knows Mia made contact with Benito. She knows I've been gone. She knows you're here looking for me."

Ann pulled out the tiny cell phone and quickly dialed a number. "It's me, I am just checking in. No nothing yet. You're probably right. He's fine. How are the children? And the others? I see. I'll call when I know something," she ended the call and quickly dialed another.

"Joshua, where is Sonja? When? And the others? Where are the children? Joshua, leave the house. Take them someplace safe. I don't know. Get a hotel room. Don't tell me where. Just do it and call me when you're there. Assume you are being followed. Take every precaution," she ended the call and the moment she did, it rang. "It's Sonja". She said staring at the phone. She hesitated but answered on the fourth ring.

"No, we're still in Auckland," she said after pause. We decided to spend the day here. No, David was exhausted after the trip. We will," she ended the call. Her expression was dark. "She left the church shortly after we did. She led me to believe she was still there. She lied to me.

"She's coming, mom. We don't have much time."

"Alright Sean, let's go," she said.

"The hotel," he said. His body began the dramatic shift into the same beastly form I had seen on the road that night. The change was complete before his hands hit the ground and he bounded off in the direction of Nelligan's Rail stop.

"Sam?" Ann said.

"On my way ma'am," Sam said as he turned and ran back toward the Rover.

"Let's go, David," she said.

It felt incredible to move that fast. The cool air became cold and thrilled me as I cut through the night close behind Ann. I could see Sean clearly ahead of her, sprinting hand and foot to the ground, covering great distances with each powerful leap. He broke through the tree line with one final explosive leap and landed on his feet in human form in the middle of the street. We halted at the tree line. He turned and motioned for us to continue. As we stepped into the street in front of the old hotel I saw a single dark figure standing in the window of a dimly lit room on the second floor. Sean nodded to the dark figure and the curtain fell in from of the window obscuring whoever it was from view.

Moments later the sound of the Rover's over revved engine preceded the sound of screeching tires as Sam rounded the curve into town and came to an abrupt stop opposite the hotel. He quickly exited the car and ran to join us in the street.

"Did I miss anythin'?" he asked as he caught his breath. Neither of us spoke a word; we just looked back to Sean.

"It's ok, mom," he said.

We crossed the street and entered the small lobby of the hotel, which was completely deserted. A single lamp burned on the high front desk. We moved slowly up the stairs to the second floor. Not a single sound could be heard in the place. The hallway was long, narrow and the only light came from widely spaced, single bulb light fixtures. Sean stopped at room number 37. We all stood behind him as he knocked one single knock on the old wooden door. The knob turned and the door began to open. Soft yellow light spilled out into the hallway as the door slowly opened.

"Hello David," she said. The shock was almost more than I could bear.

T. S. Worley

Chapter Six

Hatred stirs up dissension, but love covers over all wrongs.
Proverbs 10:12

Seeing her there, the realization that she was part of it all. It was a miserable feeling. I thought I had gotten over her. I thought I was over losing her but I wasn't. A deep ache welled inside me like I had been punched in the gut and I could smell the iron in the bloody tears forming in my own eyes.

"Sarah?" I managed to whisper.

I felt it happening. I was going to black out again. I passively wondered if it would ever stop happening as the walls began to tilt. The reassuring grasp of competent hands was the last thing I was aware of before darkness filled my vision.

***

I was sitting on a bench in a beautiful garden. Flowers were in bloom everywhere the eye came to rest. The air was heavy with their sweet fragrance. I expected to see the old man sitting at my side but I was alone. I scanned the area around me for any sign of him but I was hesitant to leave the bench. I sat there for as long as I could tolerate and decided to explore the dreamscape. I was about to stand up when I felt a hand on my shoulder.

"Don't get up David, It's alright. I'll join you. Were you looking for someone?" he asked. He startled me, caught me off guard. I was too busy assessing him to answer his question. There was something familiar about him; something about his elegant voice alarmed me. He sat next to on the bench.

"Do you find it pleasing?" he asked as he gestured to the environment with smooth fluid movements.

"Who are you?" I asked. He smiled and laughed light fluttery laugh.

"David, don't you know? Haven't you sorted it all out yet? I'm disappointed in you. I thought you were brighter than that," he said condescendingly. I stood up and moved away from him instinctively. "Now David, I mean you no harm," he said as if speaking to a child.

"Where's the old man?" I asked.

"He is distracted for the moment. This little meeting is just between the two of us, David," he answered slyly.

"Is this a dream?" I asked.

"It's an opportunity," he answered.

"An opportunity for what?" I asked.

"An opportunity for you to hear what I have to say," he answered.

"I'm a captive audience, aren't I?" I asked in response to his vaguely sarcastic tone.

"Oh David let's not get on this way. We don't have a great deal of time. I can't keep you here forever. Let's not spend what time we have squabbling. Now listen and I won't fill your head with puzzles and riddles. I'll make this easy for you to understand. I am what you would call the Devil, David. Lucifer, Satan, the Adversary."

I was afraid and it showed. I backed further away from him without thinking, though I had nowhere to run.

"Don't be afraid. Forget what you know, David. I'm not the boogieman. Ultimately; he and I have the same goal. It's all in how you get there. The devil is in the details as they say.

Let me put it to you this way: Pain and suffering, sadness, loneliness; David, I want a world without any of those things. In my world there would be no pain, no loss. Everyone would love and be loved. No death or sickness. For want of that I have been an outcast, a troubled child. Ask yourself, David. Is free agency worth it?"

***

"Mate. Mate, are you alright?" Sam asked as the room quickly came into focus. I was thirsty, very thirsty.

"Ann" I called out.

"I'm here, David," she said as she helped me stand.

"I have to drink. Now, "I said urgently.

"Sam. My bag," she said.

"Got it ma'am," he said and he flew from the room.

Sarah stood looking out the only window in the room. Her arms were folded tightly about her chest. She looked sad and forlorn. But she was still so beautiful. I wanted to ask her a million questions but I could barely contain the thirst. I didn't dare move or even speak.

A few moments later Sam returned with a worn leather bag. From it, Ann produced one of the familiar silver cylinders. She removed the top quickly and handed it to me. I poured its contents down my throat greedily. Instantly the thirst began to ebb away. I could think clearly again. My thoughts became my own. I became aware of the two others in the room. Sean and another man stood in the small kitchen. The man's back was to me and he was speaking at a whisper too softly for even my improved ears to hear. Sean nodded occasionally, looking from him to the floor to me.

"Better?" Ann asked.

"Better," I answered. At that the other man and Sean ended their almost silent conversation and Sarah turned her attention from the window to me. Ann moved between the other man and I like a statue and took a stance like an angry lioness.

"Give me a reason not to tear you apart," she said harshly.

"Is that any way to greet an old friend, Aiana?" he asked.

"Cut to the chase Benito!" she responded.

"Marcus?!" I exclaimed. "Marcus Bennett?!" I said again. "This is Benito?! Marcus, you're Benito? You son of a bitch!" I yelled.

"What the Hell is going on?" Ann exclaimed. The situation became extremely volatile for a moment but it was Sarah that broke the tension.

"She would have killed me, David," she said. "Sonja, she would have killed me. Marcus saw it. That's why I left."

"Sarah, are you one of them?" I asked desperately. The sweet musky scent permeated everything in the room. I couldn't discern her scent from anyone else's.

"Since long before we met," she answered as she looked to the floor.

"I can't believe this, I roared. I'm losing my freaking mind!" I screamed.

"David, Stop it," Sarah said. "It's me. I'm the same woman you fell in love with. I never meant to hurt you."

"Never meant to hurt me?! I am beyond hurt. I feel like I'm stark raving mad! You took my whole world away. I loved you! Things were perfect and one day it was all gone. You were gone. You left with no explanation, no good bye, not even a Dear John letter. Nothing. I came to see you at the airport and you just looked right through me. And that big scene at the apartment with Marcus, or Benito or whoever the hell he is, "I shouted pointing at Marcus.

"What was all that about?! Jesus Christ, Sarah!" I ranted. Everyone in the room fell silent. I fell silent.

"I'm sorry. I just don't understand any of this. I feel very, very crazy, "I said.

"David, I hope that you will forgive me one day for what I, for what we did. It is true. She never meant to hurt you. We never meant to hurt you. There is a much bigger picture that you must see. Think about your life, David. I know you feel that you have suffered much, and I see that you have but has it not also been a charmed life, David. Have you ever been sick, have you ever had so much as a cold? No. And think back. How many close calls have you had? How many times have you escaped harm or injury?

You have had a dark angel at your side, David. But that same angel has wrought destruction in your life as well. She took your parents from you. She systematically orchestrated your isolation. She chose the time and place to manifest this change in you. David she has held your life in her hands since before you were born. She has tended your family tree for generations."

As I listened to him I thought about the events of my life that defied explanation. In retrospect there were a number of times when I felt more than lucky. I wondered if it were possible that she had been there without my knowing it. I knew that I could nearly move faster than the human eye could perceive. Maybe she was faster.

"Why should we believe you?" Ann asked.

"Ask for yourself, David. Ask God to reveal the truth to you." Marcus said. I considered sharing the nature of the dreams I'd been having but I changed my mind just before the words crossed my tongue.

"I see," he said with a smile. "He has already begun to show you," he continued. "But there is another voice in your head."

"What are you doing?" I asked.

"It is a gift we have, David. We catch the thoughts of others. It is difficult and sometimes it is hard to sort out the thoughts from your own, but I hear you well enough," he said.

"Can you do it too Sarah, can you hear my thoughts?" I asked.

"Yes David, I can. I'm so sorry," she replied.

"You always knew exactly what to say and did exactly what I wanted. Now I know why. I thought you were perfect for me but you were just playing me the whole time," she didn't answer. She went to the window and hugged herself tightly as she looked out. I thought how beautiful she looked even when she was sad. She smiled a brief, pained smile.

"I never knew you possessed that ability." Ann said.

"I never told you. I never told any of you." Marcus said. It nearly drove me mad and when the others came it worsened. There were so many voices. In time I was able to sort them out and when I did, Sonja's thoughts betrayed her, Aiana. I had to leave. The stories she shared. The life she claims to have lived. Lies, it's all lies. Oh there are bits and pieces of truth woven in here and there, just enough to make you want to believe her. But it's a lie just the same. I wanted to tell you Aiana. But I heard your thoughts as well. You were loyal to a fault. You would never have believed me. Leaving was the only choice I had and the church was my only refuge. Of course I had to reveal my secret to them. I had to reveal you're existence as well.

It was a terrible time for me. Pope Alexander was truly a tyrant. He starved me, beat me, deprived me of sleep; he forced me to deliver the curse unto him. It's true, Sonja did come. But she came to kill me. She encountered the wolf Pope instead. The details of their dealings are unknown to me but her claim that the church killed him from within are untrue. She killed him and all that he spawned. If she had known my location she would have killed me as well.

Werewolves were merely an anomaly to her, something she could use or destroy as she saw fit.

Then there was the child, the vampire child. I have seen it in my nightmares. Torn from its mother's womb at the hands of my kind. It was then she began to eradicate us. She made her army. She purged the world of werewolves. She allowed me to live out of curiosity alone. She wanted to observe me, study me. She was ever the scientist. Even then. But when the moment came that she could no longer control me it was then that I outlived my usefulness. I saw it in my mind. She planned to kill me. I chose the hour I could best escape and I fled. But I'm talking in circles Aiana. Seeing you again has brought back so many memories. I have missed you so," he said.

"Why was the child destroyed Benito?" Ann asked as her face darkened.

"It was an abomination Aiana. This child she is so desperate to bring about. It would be the destroyer of worlds. Its birth would mean the end of mankind. It would mean the end for us all," he answered gravely. At hearing that, out of a long forgotten instinct, Ann gasped as if the wind had been knocked out of her.

"How do you know that?" I asked.

"I have seen it, David. I have seen its birth. This must not come to fruition," he replied.

"You could be wrong." Ann interjected. "You could be lying."

"If I were then why would she be coming here?" he asked.

"How do you know she is?" she asked.

"I see her," he answered, "I see her now; I see her searching the city for you."

"David, please believe us," Sarah pleaded.

"Believe you? Why should I believe you? Everything you said and did was a lie!" I replied bitterly.

"Not everything, David. Not everything. No one forced me to love you. No one forced me to do anything. I chose to be in your life. I wanted to be there. David I loved you with all my heart. I knew every day that if she discovered me it would be the end of my life. I didn't want to leave but when Marcus told what he had seen, I had no choice. I had to go. Please understand that," she pleaded.

"David, we wanted to bring you in. We had hoped to make you one of us. We tried but you were not ready. Your mind was not open to it. When Sonja closed in, we had to get Sarah out of there." Marcus said. "I apologize for the manner in which it was carried out but I wanted you to be angry. I did not want you to follow her. Be angry with me, David. Not Sarah," he added.

"What makes you think I'm NOT angry with you, Marcus?" I said through clinched teeth. I wanted to hurt him. I wanted to rip him apart with my bare hands. I could feel my anger growing by the second. The smell of them filled my flared nostrils and threatened to drive me insane.

"Stop it, David. Just stop it!" Sarah screamed. "You want to hurt someone, hurt me!" She growled as she shifted into her wolf form and closed the distance between us.

I didn't see her move she crossed the room so quickly, my vampire vision couldn't even keep up with her. But in an instant Sarah was no longer in front of me. Ann had intercepted her and thrown her against the wall. Sarah pounced on Ann, slamming her to the floor. The floorboards split with the impact. It all happened in fractions of seconds. Without thinking I moved to pull Sarah off of her. I grabbed her by the shoulders and pulled her from the floor. She snarled as she spun into my arms, shifting fluidly back into the beautiful girl I loved so much, before she fell into me, wrapping her arms around me and pressing her face to my chest. She was sobbing openly.

"I am so sorry, David. I never stopped loving you. Please believe me," she pleaded. I closed my eyes and let the warmth of her embrace fill a painful void that had remained unhealed since the day she walked out the door. I do still love her, I thought as I returned her embrace. I opened my eyes to see Ann lying frozen on the damaged floor, a look of grief in her eyes. She loves me too I thought.

"Are you ok, Mom?" Sean asked helping her to her feet.

"I'm fine," she said. I'm just fine."

Sam had plastered himself to the door leading from the room. Obviously terrified by the brief but violent exchange. Marcus had not moved. He stood unmoved by the conflict, except that he seemed to be praying. His eyes were closed and his head bowed. He was murmuring the faintest whispered chant. I couldn't make out what it was he was saying but Sarah responded to him.

"I'm sorry, Marcus," she said sadly.

"It's alright my child. You could have done nothing to prevent it. It was unavoidable. Are you alright?" he asked without opening his eyes.

"I am now," she answered.

"Aiana, she has left the city. She will go to the remains of the chapel at Lake Tepako. From there she will travel directly to our location. We have very little time. She will come for her David," he said.

"Why me! I keep asking and no one has given me an answer that fits. Everything just raises more questions, "I said.

"It's quite simple, David. You are the last in your line. The last to carry the traits she requires to complete her mission. And she has chosen Ann to be your bride," he said. Ann knew all of that. I knew she knew it.

"Do any of the others know what she has done? Are they with her?" Ann asked.

"I suspect at least two of them are involved. I believe the others are merely your potential replacements should you fail to produce an offspring. You are, I believe, expendable to her. She will kill us all except you, David," he said.

"She has to know that I wouldn't cooperate with this, "I said.

"David, there are, how shall I say, less romantic methods she could employ to get what she wants." Marcus answered.

"Mother, we have to go," Sean urged.

"I'm with Sean, with all that ruckus someone's bound ta come lookin," Sam said.

"The building is empty," Sarah said.

"Right, off-season," Sam added. Ann pulled the tiny cell phone from her pocket and keyed in a number. After a moment she ended the call and replaced the phone in her pocket.

"She didn't answer," she said. The phone rang back seconds later. "Hello?" she answered. The room fell silent. I could hear the voice on the other end as clearly as if she were in the room.

"Forgive me child, I was on the other line. I must meet with the board of ethics, apparently there are concerns about some of the testing going on at the lab and I want to address them as quickly as possible. How are you? Is David alright, Have you learned any news of Sean," Sonja asked.

"He's fine. I didn't tell you earlier, I'm sorry we left without telling you." Ann answered.

"It is alright young one, I do understand," Sonja replied.

"I found him, Sonja. He's here with me." Ann said flatly.

"That is wonderful news child! Praise be to God!" Sonja exclaimed. An uneasy dread filled the room as each listener's eyes shifted from one to another.

"And so is Benito," she added.

"I see," Sonja replied.

"I have to ask you, Sonja. Where are you now, really?" Ann asked. A long silence followed the question.

"I would speak to David now," she said.

"He can hear you," Ann replied. All eyes turned to me.

"David, you cannot escape me," she said. Her voice was no longer warm and melodious. It was menacing and cruel. "Run, David and I will find you. And when I do, you will suffer. But if you tell me now, where you are, I will spare you the horror of watching me tear your companions apart. Just as I spared you the screams of your parents as the flesh burned from their bodies," she said. Rage swelled from deep in my soul.

"Why!" I groaned through clenched teeth, fighting back tears.

"Why, why, why, David. They were pathetic, drunks who could barely care for themselves. I simply couldn't trust them with your care. After all, I couldn't be there every moment of every day," she said with casual disdain.

I had always suffered so much guilt for surviving that fire. I had night terrors when I was a child and I would sleep walk almost nightly. The night of the fire I had been awakened in the dew covered grass by the sounds of sirens. I had always thought I had been sleep walking and happened to make it outside by chance. But now I know my dark angel laid me gently in the grass.

"You psychotic bitch!" I screamed. Laughter emanated from the phone.

"Oh David, I'm much worse than that." The call ended. I wanted to hit something, destroy something.

"We have to leave this place, David," Marcus said placing his heavy hand on my shoulder. That was just what I needed. The crack of my fist connecting with his jaw sounded like a rifle report but he took it like a sturdy oak.

"I suppose I had that coming," he said righting himself and messaging his incorruptible jaw. "May we go now?" he asked wryly.

107

"Let's get the hell out of here," I said. Everyone voiced his or her agreement but Ann. She was visibly shaken.

"I didn't know, David. I've been so foolish. How could I have not known? She's the devil isn't she?" Ann asked. She seemed dysphonic and detached. She wasn't asking me so much as she was letting it sink in. I just listened; the others had assembled outside the door in the hallway. "I have to stop her," she added. "You have to go, all of you, now," she continued. "I will slow her down, I can't stop her but I can buy you enough time to get away."

"Mom, no!" Sean shouted as he stormed back into the room. "I won't let you do that," he said desperately.

"No, I won't either" I said. "Listen, we do not have time to stand here debating the issue, she could be here at any moment. "We all go."

"Agreed," Sarah said. Ann nodded reluctantly. And we all made for the stairs.

"Listen, mates. I don't wanna sound lik a coward but I don't think I can keep up with the lot of ya," Sam said as he ran down the stairs taking several at a time.

"Do not worry, my young friend. You will not be left behind. You will drive to the Bluff as fast as you can. The others will go with you while I confuse her scent. I will meet you at South Port. A ship is waiting. Sarah will take you to it." Marcus said. We climbed into the Rover and Sam slid into the driver's seat.

"Fasten ya seat...nevamind," he said.

"Be careful, Marcus," Sarah said.

"God speed, Benito," Ann wished him. He smiled and winked as he closed the door. His smile distorted slightly and in an instant he shifted his form and vanished from sight.

Sam started the engine and slammed the accelerator to the floor. The supercharged V8 roared into action and we were on our way south to the coast. It was in the predawn hours when we reached the Bluff. Silence had been the preferred method of travel, save for the occasional colorful expletive erupting from Sam as he tried to navigate the torturous highways without losing speed. Sarah directed us down highway one through Invercargill, across the port highway to the sprawling South Port complex.

It seemed a bit eerie on the deserted dock. The ship she guided us to wasn't at all what I was expecting. The cargo ship Perseverance, a cold silent behemoth, sat waiting. We sat in the Rover with engine and lights off listening to nothing but the sound of the engine popping as it cooled and the sound of water lapping the side of the massive steel hull of the ship. There was no sign of Marcus. There was no sign of anyone. It was the kind of dead quiet that makes you afraid to even move. When the driver's door flung open Sam screamed a long list of swear words and claimed he soiled himself. Marcus had come out of the darkness without a sound. He was exhausted.

"Let's go, quickly!" he said between gasps for air. He shouted something in a foreign language and the ship came to life. Its massive diesel engines reverberated throughout the empty deserted port. We boarded her quickly and she began to creep slowly away from the dock. The ship was then crawling with deck hands. I thought they sounded Russian.

"Did you see her?" Ann asked.

"Only a glimpse," Marcus answered. I led her north and doubled back on my path in Wellington. I don't think she followed me south but I crossed my own trail many times. I have been here for an hour and I have not seen or heard anything until you arrived. I have tried to catch her thoughts but I cannot," he added.

The further away from the port we moved the more at ease I felt. Truth was I wanted to face her but on my own terms. For the moment, we all felt as though we had made a clean escape. Days would pass before we learned of the destruction and horror she unleashed on the small crew who maintained night operations at the port. As we sailed off into the night, Sonja was obtaining the destination of our next port of call amidst the screams of the poor terror stricken souls at Port Bluff.

The scent of wolves was almost stifling onboard the hulking transport, even in the open sea air of the deck. I quickly realized we were being ferried away by an entire pack of werewolves. Tension and apprehension hung like a thick fog all about the ship. Marcus led us all into the stark, steel interior of the vessel where the ship's captain, a wiry old sea dog by the name of Afanos, greeted us in English. His warm manner seemed even more so in contrast to the stark surroundings. He politely provided us with utilitarian accommodations, which were the best the ship had to offer.

Ann, Sean, Sam and I crowded into the hostel like bunk room containing four meager bunks. Being on the ship reminded me of the security of being in the air. I felt at ease walled off behind the windowless steel door. Both Sam and Sean obviously felt the same way as they collapsed on their thin mattresses and issued sighs of relief. Ann didn't seem to share the same feeling.

"Are you alright?" I asked.

"No," she answered quickly. "I need to lay down," she said.

"What's wrong, Mom?" Sean asked with obvious worry in his voice. I sensed he had never seen her as anything but unwaveringly strong.

"I just need a moment to process all of this," she answered.

"C'mon mate. Let's find the galley in this tub," Sam said, giving Sean a firm slap on the shoulder. Sean reluctantly followed Sam as he set in search of food. I stood watching Ann feeling uneasy about her sudden decline.

"I'm fine, David. Really," she assured me. "I just need to gather my thoughts," she continued. She added an obligatory reassuring smile, the kind you give when you are clearly not fine but have no intention of saying otherwise.

"If you need me, I'll be close, "I said.

"You don't have a choice right now," she said with a grin.

"I can swim for it," I replied.

"No, you can't. Sorry. You aren't' buoyant anymore. You'll sink like a stone. It's a long dark walk on the sea floor to the coast," she said.

"I'm not going anywhere, Ann," I replied.

"I know, David," she closed her eyes and curled her slender frame into a ball. I closed the door and made my way up to the deck. I saw Marcus standing staring out into the predawn sky. I crossed the deck and stood beside him in silence for a moment before speaking to him.

"Sorry about the uh.., "I said, motioning my fist to my chin.

"Is nothing," he said.

"Where are you taking us?" I asked.

"This ship is carrying us all to safety but a long journey lies before us," he answered.

"Is there a safe place now?" I asked.

"Kaien Island, it's where I call home," he said. "The Pacific Northwest has been good to us. We live and thrive amongst our four legged cousins," he added.

"How long will it take to get there?" I asked.

"Two weeks' time before we reach the coast of Japan. From there, another ten days," he said. I wasn't feeling the thirst at that moment but it was never truly out of my mind. And the thought of being trapped aboard a cargo ship for fourteen days without a single drop of blood gave was cause for concern.

"It's alright David. I was prepared for this. I have a large supply of freshly frozen blood. It doesn't suit my pallet but I think it will meet your needs," he assured me.

"Ann is not well?" he said questioningly.

111

"She's upset," I answered.

"And you?" he asked.

"Why didn't you just tell me? Why all the games? I loved her, Marcus. I would have loved her no matter what," I said.

"David, I tried to tell you, Sarah tried to tell you. You wouldn't listen. You wouldn't open your mind to anything I had to say. The more I tried to tell you, the further you pulled away. Nothing I did or said changed the picture in my mind of Sarah dying by Sonja's hand and of you taking your own life after learning the truth about us," he said gravely. I shuddered at the thought of that alternate reality.

"What was will never be again, David. But Sarah loved you then and loves you now. I am no longer a man of the cloth. I abandoned the priesthood long ago and I have followed many paths since, but I am a man of God. I have given my life to Him. I will not take from any man, the life that God has given. But when you made the transformation, it was Sarah who kept you alive. You see, I convinced myself that you had abandoned the breath of life that the Almighty had filled your lungs with. I told myself He would understand, He would approve of my actions. He would forgive me for killing you in order to save humanity. It seemed a noble act, a reasonable trade. But it was Sarah who helped me see my arrogance. How could I judge your heart, your soul, and your humanity? Without offering my own for judgment. I couldn't," he said with finality.

"You'll love the island, David," he said changing the subject. "It has everything Tennessee has to offer and more. By the time we reach land you will have adjusted to our scent. And even if Sonja knew where we were going she wouldn't be able to track you among us," he added.

"Thank you, Marcus. Thank you for helping us, "I said.

"Thank Sarah," he replied.

***

Time passed slowly. The days all began to run together. Ann's sudden decline became a worsening condition. She attributed it to seasickness; she tried very hard to convince me it was one of the few ailments a vampire could suffer from.

"It's all in my head," she would say. Marcus watched her closely and as the days passed, he spent more and more time at her bedside. A place he had to share with Sean and myself. She protested vehemently to all the fuss but it was a hollow protest. She was much sicker than she allowed us to see. But she maintained that she would be fine once she set foot on dry land again.

Sam immersed himself in the activities of the crewmen. In three days' time he had befriended everyone on the ship. Sarah, however, was aloof. I saw her rarely and when I did catch a glimpse, it was of her glancing over her shoulder as she bolted in the other direction. I regretted the things I said back at the hotel and after talking to Marcus I felt even worse. I hoped for an opportunity to let her know I understood and to thank her for caring about me after all that time.

The two weeks of sailing was about to come to an end. We were nearing the city of Kobe on the Japanese seaboard. I felt a feeling of dread that night that I would never forget or ignore ever again. Ann was still clinging to her seasickness theory and was looking forward to trading in her sea legs for a bit. The entire crew; including Sam were beginning preparations for offloading the ship's cargo, lumber mostly, which had made the unusual trip to the southern hemisphere and back before reaching its final destination in Kobe. The closer we drew to the port, the more apprehensive I became. I looked to Marcus frequently but he seemed not to sense, nor see anything disturbing. If he did, it didn't show. Never the less, I shared my vague fears with Sean and asked him to help me keep watch.

The Kobe port was milling with activity when we arrived. A steady stream of shipments moved in an out at an amazing pace. Massive cranes, an army of men, loading and offloading without pause. The noise and constant movement was very distracting. I found myself wanting to stay onboard but I knew I had to get Ann off the ship if for no other reason than to confirm that something was actually wrong with her. I thought that if she would only admit it we could start trying to find out what was happening to her.

It pains me deeply to remember the events of that night. The four of us; Ann, Sean, Marcus and myself set out at a mortal stride, venturing into the city for the sole purpose of giving Ann a respite from the confines of the ship. But we never made it into the city. We didn't even make it beyond the port authority. I could ramble on about reaction times and movements far too fast to be seen by human eyes but that isn't the nature of the way the memory plays in my mind.

It was painfully slow; the mind moving so quickly, too quickly for the laws of physics that bind even us, to keep up with. After ten minutes of walking away from the ocean she hadn't shown any sign of improvement. Periodically she walked with her eyes closed and simply used one of us as a guide. She was weak and I felt she was becoming disoriented. I was more worried than ever. From the look on Sean's face he was too. I knew Marcus was concerned but he maintained a calm exterior. He was so much different to me now. He seemed so much older, so tempered. I thought of Sonja's tale of him and how she had said that he seemed old and haggard at times and youthful and vibrant at others. I wondered if it was really due to some inner struggle. I was studying him intently at the moment I saw the change flash across his face, wiping away his calm outward expression.

We should never have left the ship but I had been lulled into the notion that Marcus would have seen any danger before it came too close to us. I was mistaken. I hate how slowly it all transpired. I wish I could wipe everything from my mind. I was enthralled by each miniscule shift he made from man to wolf at a devastatingly slow rate of speed. I saw his attention shift, his body begin to take action even as it bent and stretched into the sinewy beast, werewolf. I saw confusion, regret, indecision and love in his eyes as he clenched his jaw and moved himself in front of Ann. I saw all of these things before I could blink my eyes.

My eyelids closed like a heavy curtain at the end of the show and reopened just as slowly. I saw the shock in his eyes as his magnificent body crumpled below his severed head. Meiko wielded a glimmering sword meant undoubtedly to take Ann's life. Marcus shielded her with his own body. He had given his life to save hers, though his eyes betrayed the conflict he felt in doing so.

Ann collapsed almost as quickly as he did. I caught her safely in my arms before she could reach the ground and just as the glistening steel blade came to a wavering stop inches from my face as I found myself between Meiko and her target. The blade was in my hand before I knew I was taking it and it severed her spine at the neck before she knew she had been struck. Strands of her ebony hair began a slow decent to the earth as her head rolled off of her milky white shoulders.

Sean was back to the ship with Ann in his arms before the smell of Meiko's blood could fill my nostrils as I breathed deeply to cry out into the night. Twice now I had taken life, one from each side of the conflict. I hated it. And what's more I hated that I stood there, sword in hand, prepared to take another. I hungered to see Sonja. I yearned for satisfaction and I feared I was losing myself to bitterness I had long forgotten. But there was no satisfaction to be had that night. There was only empty, senseless loss. Marcus, the man, lay at my feet. All signs of the monster within him had evaporated in the night.

The great horn of the cargo ship sounded. I could hear Sean's voice beckoning me to come.

"The blade work is done, Vurdalak." The old gray captain said as he gently lowered the sword with his leathered hands. He had been watching us depart from the deck and reached my side as their blood mingled warm upon the ground but too slowly to affect the outcome. "Get back to her," he said as he motioned to the ship. Two hard faced deck hands sprinted to his side. Grief stricken, they carried the lifeless body of Marcus back aboard the ship. I loosed my grip on the weapon, allowing it to fall with a sharp clang. "Go!" he said urgently.

I ran back to the ship and into the small bunkroom. Ann was unconscious. Sean had placed her on her bed and was trying desperately to wake her. From somewhere below I heard a long agonizing wail. It echoed through the steel vessel from bow to stern. The sorrowful howl originated somewhere deep inside Sarah's soul when she laid eyes on the empty shell that was once Father Benito Maresca and the man I knew as Marcus Bennett.

The engines fired and the bulkheads shook. Ann lay motionless on the bunk as the ship powered away from the dock at full throttle. She looked like a beautiful corpse from some grim fairy tale. Sean was on the verge of insanity, he begged her over and over to be okay and he cried to God, asking why Marcus had to die. He blamed himself and swore on his life that he would kill Sonja. His sorrow brought tears to my own eyes.

I wasn't sure how to help Ann but I did the only thing I could think of. I gnashed my wrist and let the blood drip onto her pale mouth. She stirred, her mouth opened, and she clasped the wound with her delicate lips. She drank. She didn't open her eyes or speak. But she drank. At least that was something.

Sean calmed a bit. Sam was at the door moments later.

"Sarah needs ya, mate," he said softly to Sean. He wiped the tears from his eyes and avoided eye contact as he left the room with Sam to comfort Sarah. I could still hear her moans echo through the corridors as Ann continued to drink slowly. It was almost as if she wouldn't have had the energy to drink if gravity wasn't filling her mouth for her.

Gradually, over the next few days the force of her drink increased and she began to moan whenever my blood was not flowing freely into her mouth. My own thirst increased dramatically to keep pace with her drain on me. I tried to give her the packaged blood directly but she wouldn't respond to it. Eventually, I became locked into a constant parasitic relationship. In my inability to leave the room, Sam and Sean catered to my growing needs. None of us knew if it was helping her but it was what she needed. The more she drank the weaker I became. My own metabolism coupled with the non-stop blood loss was too much in the end. After six days, on the brink of death, I collapsed.

***

"You had to spoil our little secret didn't you, David. Do you have any idea what I have to endure from that miserable old fool?" The words dripped sickeningly rich and sweet from his tongue like molasses from an old mahogany spoon. He appeared just as before. Tailored white suit, perfect hair and a very genteel manner.

"Where are we?" I asked. The room was empty, windowless. Four plaster walls and a wood floor. A single bulb hung from the ceiling and illuminated the small empty room.

"I don't have time for all that. No distractions, David. Just listen. I have moments at best. Forget the whole good versus evil. I'm the bad guy and he's the good guy. The world doesn't work that way. It isn't black and white. It isn't even shades of gray. There are billions of colors, hues,

117

and shades. My point is that what is right and what is wrong can become very unclear sometimes. Sometimes the wrong thing brings about the right outcome. Good people do bad things. It's all jumbled up, David. The whole problem is choice.

"I know it is scary to think about having your choices taken away but what has mankind done with that ability, really? Would you not stop a murderer from killing if you could? Would you not take away his choice? And what about the mother who abused him so as a child, turning him into the monster he is? Would you take away her choice? And what of her parents, who simply didn't show their love. What about their choice? David, I want peace and happiness I just..."

***

I awoke in agony. The crushing desire for blood was more intense than it had ever been.

"Blood! Hurry!" I screamed. It was the worst feeling I could imagine. It was more than a physical need. It was a lust, a desire that demanded satisfaction one way or another. I feared for those around me and feared for my own sanity. I sensed I was very near the edge of an abyss from which there was no return.

Sean tore into one of the few remaining bags from the carefully laid provisions, allowing it to spill into my mouth. I tore it from his hands and sloppily consumed its still cold contents.

"More!" I shouted. Another bag and then another. I consumed more and more, blind to anything but the drink. After five pints I began to regain control. I opened my eyes to see Sean and Sam standing over me, both splashed in the blood of my frenzy, looks of shock and disbelief in their eyes. Sarah stood over Ann, her wrist held firmly to Ann's mouth.

"I wasn't sure if she would drink from me," Sarah said meekly. "But she doesn't seem to mind," she added. Ann steadily swallowed as Sarah's blood flowed forth. "She nearly killed you, David," Sarah said as she looked at me briefly before turning her attention back to Ann. "You can't care for her alone. She needs more than you can give. She is feeding for two now," she added.

"What do you mean?" I asked.

"Marcus told me. He knew right away. He told me in silent whispers back at the hotel. She is pregnant, David. She is carrying the child. He knew and he died to protect her. I don't know why. I don't know if he had another vision or had some realization at the last moment but he knew she was going to die.

"He knew Sonja would not allow Ann to bear the child once she betrayed her. He was resolved to allow the problem to resolve itself then keep you safe and hidden for as long as he could, forever if need be. I don't know why he changed his mind but for whatever reason, he wanted her to live," she choked back tears as she spoke. "So I have to make sure she lives too. I have to believe he knew what he was doing," she said as the tears broke through and her unwounded hand caressed Ann's hair gently.

We were all thunderstruck but no one more than I was. I didn't know what to think or say. I rose from the floor, wiped my face and sat beside Ann on the bed. I ran the gamut of emotion but foremost I was worried. Knowing what was wrong with her didn't help after all. It certainly wasn't starting out like a normal human pregnancy and no one could possibly know if this was normal for a vampire. A thousand scenarios ran through my mind with no way of sorting the rational from the irrational.

Sean crouched in the floor holding his head in his hands in silence while Sam stood there not knowing what to do. None of us did. So there we stayed in silence for almost an hour.

"I'm getting woozy," Sarah said.

"Here, let me," I said.

119

"No. Not yet," she answered. It's too dangerous.

"I'll do it," Sean said boldly. "She's my mom. I'll do it," he added. "Sam, Give me your knife". Sam handed over a large scuba knife and Sean sliced a narrow opening in his arm. Blood began to drip onto the floor. It fired my own thirst but I was ok. I could maintain. Sarah removed her wrist from Ann's mouth and she began to moan immediately. Sean quickly replaced the fount with his source as rivulets of blood ran down his forearm. She resumed the rhythmic swallowing as soon as the blood touched her lips.

"David I need to speak to you alone," Sarah said. She walked out the door without waiting for me to acknowledge. I followed her down the long corridor to an empty storeroom. "We have a problem, David," she whispered.

"What is it?" I asked.

"Marcus was going to allow Meiko to kill her. He could never have taken her life but he felt he had no choice but to stand aside. He told no one he was going to do anything other than that. Every werewolf knows the prophecy. Every werewolf only knows that Marcus believed this child would mean the destruction of mankind, the end of the world. They all believed him. David, everyone on this ship is a werewolf," she said urgently.

"Oh shit," I said in an alarmed whisper.

"If or when someone finds out, she will be in grave danger. I don't know how we could protect her," she said.

"We just have to make sure no one finds out, "I replied. We walked back down the corridor to the bunkroom where Ann was now confined by her condition. "Where's Sam?" I asked with alarm when I saw he was no longer in the room.

"He had to get some air," Sean said softly.

"Son of a..," "I didn't finish as I bolted from the room with vampiric speed. Once up top I quickly scanned the deck for Sam. Hoping to catch him before he let the big news escape his lips. But it was too late. He was already talking to his new werewolf friends and I could see his lips forming the word baby as he stood scratching his head. The two deck hands looked from one to the other, then to me. Then they were no longer a couple of deckhands. They were predators on the scent of a kill.

As I ran back to the bunkroom I looked behind me to see an entire pack of werewolves closing in on me. I exploded through the doorway and slammed the steel door shut behind me. Before I could warn Sarah and Sean the force of the pack hitting the locked door sent my flying into the opposite wall. I sprang to my feet slammed my body into the opening door, forcing it closed.

Sean the wolf stood next to me in seconds, roaring as he forced his muscled shoulder into the door. A beastly arm crashed through the small window and a ghastly cry issued forth from the other side of the door as Sean wrenched it free from its owner's possession. The hinges then gave way and the door became nothing more than a shield that we struggled to block the opening with. Arms and gnashing teeth quickly filled every opening. There seemed to be no way to hold them back. We were strong enough to hold our ground but the door was not. It was folding in around us. A few minutes more and they would flood passed us, filling the room.

Sarah stood like a mythic sentinel over an all but lifeless body, preordained to stem the tide or drown in a river of her own kind. They were coming through. I sunk the fingers on my left hand into the doorframe, trying to bridge the gaping opening. A set of powerful jaws clamped down hard on my arm. There was no pain but instead I felt an exhilarating tingling sensation rush through my body as massive teeth hit bone. Absent was the reflex to draw away.

I held firm. I would not have let them in while I still had strength to resist. But I was already weak and I was beginning to falter. I doubt I could have held up another minute. The shot ringing out came not a moment too soon. It was followed quickly by the voice of Afanos.

"Stop! All of you! Have you lost your minds?" he demanded with his booming voice. The attack halted immediately. The obedient pack quickly dispersed and the door slammed to the floor. The old captain stepped through the emptied doorway, holstering his side arm as he did so. "It's for the getting of attention only," he said. "Bullets mean nothing to us," he added. "Sarah, I apologize. I do not have the clarity of sight I once had. I thought we would be at home before anyone else had to know."

"You know? He told you?" she asked.

"The night he went ashore, just before he left the ship. He gave me this letter to give to you," he replied as he produced a folded envelope from his pocket. He handed it to Sarah tenderly. The old man had an easy manner in spite of his rough exterior. Sarah took the letter and opened it slowly, carefully unfolding it as if it were some ancient parchment that might crumble in uncaring hands. She read it aloud.

"My dearest Sarah, I am sorry, but I knew you would try to prevent me from doing what must be done. You see, I have had another vision. And your time in this world is not yet finished. I know now however, mine at long last has come to an end. The Lord of Heaven has called me home. Sarah, I have seen the birth of the child once more. But God has shown me a bringer of peace, a messenger of hope. Not the destroyer of worlds as I have seen before. The future is not set in stone, each decision; each action tips the scale with each passing moment. Hope lives within us all. It is difficult to understand the will of God at times but I know now this must be. And so I must ensure that Ann will live long enough to bare her child, even at the cost of my own life. There must be free will. There must be choice.

The truth is hope, the truth is light and it is never compelled. Protect her. See her through. Take care of David. Take care of the child. I love you so much, my darling sister."

I had been so ignorant. It became so clear to me. If only I hadn't been blinded by my own fears and insecurities, I might have listened to Marcus in the beginning but instead I was filled with jealousy and distrust. She refolded it slowly and placed it into her pants pocket as tears pooled in her rich brown eyes.

"I can't do this," she whispered through gentle sobs.

"You can child. You must. You are not alone child. Marcus gave his very life to save the child. I don't understand the why. But he devoted his life to God and to all of us. If he believed this to be the will of the Lord of Heaven, then we will obey. You have a lot of work to do child. We are sailing into Kaien in three days. What happened here only moments ago is but a taste of the reception we face ahead. We have a lot of minds to change." The old captain said as he placed his weathered hands on her shoulders and bent close to look into her watery eyes.

"Be strong Sarah," he added, then turned and limped hurriedly out of the room. A steady stream of Russian thundered from his mouth as he made his way down the corridor.

"Why didn't you tell me, Sarah?" I asked.

"I wanted to, but by the time things started going bad, it was too late. Sonja came back and we had to leave. And when I saw you again, I wanted to but then there was..." she trailed off and didn't finish the thought but I understood as she looked to Ann.

"He's right, Sarah," Sean interrupted, having shifted back into his boyish human form. "What are we going to do?" he asked.

"I don't know, Sean. I don't know what to do anymore," she answered.

"I have to find my brothers. They need to know," Sean said more to himself than to us.

Ann began to moan again. I wondered if she were aware of the danger she had been in only minutes ago. She seemed to be oblivious to anything but the thirst. Sarah wiped her eyes as she sat on the side of the bed and was just about to place her wrist to Ann's yearning lips when she leapt from the bed.

"David!" she exclaimed as she pulled back the rough olive drab blanket that had been concealing her body.

"My God," I whispered. Her abdomen had swollen remarkably.

"I sensed him!" she said, leaning close as she pulled her long dark hair aside to inspect the rapid change in Ann's body. She leapt back again with a gasp. "It's a boy. David, you're going to have a son. And I think he's aware of us. He knows. I've never felt anything like this before," she whispered. Her eyes were wide with wonder as she shuddered and rubbed her arms briskly as if to ward off the cold.

"Are you okay?" I asked.

"I'm fine," she answered

"Are you sure it's a boy?" I asked.

"Yes, I'm certain," she answered as she sat back down on the side of the bed and gently placed her bare wrist against Ann's waiting lips. Sarah gave a brief moan as Ann bit into her delicate flesh.

"It's okay Ann. I understand now. I won't let anything happen to him. None of us will," she whispered softly as she gently brushed away the strands of hair that crossed Ann's face.

"I can't explain it David, but everything is going to be ok," she said softly.

"Why is it happening so fast? What's it doing to her?" Sean asked.

"I don't know. But I think he is going to come very soon," Sarah replied.

"I have to find Joshua," Sean said.

"The captain has a satellite phone," Sarah answered. And with that Sean quickly left the room in search of Captain Afanos.

"I understand why you had to go, Sarah," I said.

"I know," she replied. "Get some rest and nourishment. She will need you soon. I'm already getting woozy."

I was thirsty and weak so I did as she suggested. I went to the storage room where the provisions were kept. There was very little blood left. I only hoped Sarah and the others would be able to sustain Ann and I wondered what we would face when we reached port. How would we feed? Where would we stay? What would happen with Ann and my...my son?

My life had changed so quickly, the entire world as I knew it had changed. And things were still changing. After Sarah left I had vowed I would never have children. And suddenly I was faced with the reality of having a son. And not just a son, he was to be a being that had never walked the earth before. And he was killing Ann. I cared for her. And I knew she loved me for what I was. For what my existence meant to her. She believed in this child in spite of Sonja's deceit, in spite of Marcus's warnings. I think she knew that bringing the child into the world would be the death of her and yet she walked to her destiny selflessly.

And then there was Sarah. She was the only woman I had allowed myself to love. And when she went away it left more than a little hole in me. It emptied me. I had nothing to give to anyone once she was gone. And now here she was, suddenly thrust into my world again. And the dreams, they were like some quiet power struggle going on inside my head.

Life had been in constant flux since that day in the park and I was struggling to keep it all in check. I dreaded arriving at Kaien. I didn't know where Sarah's new found optimism came from but I didn't share it and obviously the werewolves were passionate in their beliefs and to them, this child meant destruction to not only them but to all of mankind. The Captain had managed to convince those aboard but how many were there? I tried not to think about it. But for the first time in a long time I found myself willing to pray.

Chapter Seven

Precious in the sight of the LORD is the death of his saints.
Psalm 116:15

The next three days were grueling. Ann's thirst increased more than I thought possible. And her pregnancy advanced just as quickly. If I hadn't known any better I would say she were nine months pregnant. She had exhausted Sean, Sarah and myself and on the last day Sam had to step in and relieve us, which he did without complaint. I could tell he felt sorry for what had happened. He meant no harm by telling the crew about the pregnancy but he was very contrite just the same.

I was too fatigued to worry about or even notice we were arriving at Kaien Island. It was pouring rain when we docked. The captain had two deck hands gently move Ann to an old stretcher and they carried her to shore with Afanos limping along briskly beside us. We were making our way to an old red pick-up truck, which looked strained under the weight of a large camper shell on the back. Before we left the ship, Afanos told us that a woman by the name of Mouge would be picking us up and taking us to a cabin in a remote corner of the island, far from humans and werewolves alike and that Sean's human siblings were already there and waiting.

Sarah knew Mouge and seemed to have mixed feelings about the decision. As we neared the truck, an old woman with long silver streaked hair and shawl covered shoulders hobbled out of the cab around to the back of the truck. She opened the tail gate and motioned for us to hurry.

"Come on now. Let's go. The deck hands slid the stretcher into back of the truck and the rest of us climbed in on either side of her. Sarah was about to climb in when the old woman caught her by the arm. "No, no. In the cab, little one," she said. Sarah hesitated looking to Ann who was beginning to moan again. "They'll tend to her. I don't like this one bit. You better have a lot to say. Cause I got a lot of questions needs answering," she added.

Sarah closed us in with a slam of the tailgate and climbed into the cab beside Mouge. The old truck rattled to life and lurched forward. Sam struggled to hold his position as he squatted in the upper corner of the truck bed. Ann moaned desperately in response to the sudden movement. We all instinctively moved to ease her ever-present thirst. I had run out of blood the day before and had given all I had taken in to Ann the following night. I was empty and thirsty myself, and the others knew it.

"I'll do it," Sam said. "I'm up for it," he added. He then placed his wrist against her mouth. He looked away as she bit into his flesh and clasped the wound with her parched mouth.

The truth was none of us were up to it. All of us were sunken, haggard and hollow. I couldn't imagine the four of us alone would be able to sustain her very much longer. I hoped Sarah was right and he did come soon. The pregnancy was killing us all.

I listened over the road noise and the sound of the engine to Sarah recounting recent events to the old woman, including the sacrifice Marcus made, without interruption.

We went through the town center and out again, down winding paved roads to gravel and dirt. Clay mud slung up and thudded against the underside of the truck as we drove down a rough pothole scarred logging road.

Sam became spent and moments from unconsciousness. I had to pull him free before he bled completely out. His pulse was rapid and thready. He fell against me and the scent of him drove me mad. His heart beating against me, the bloody wounds on his wrist. It was more than I could tolerate. I had to drink. And I had to do it fast.

"Take him, "I said to Sean as I piled his limp, exhausted body into Sean's arms. "I have to get out of here, "I said.

Sarah wheeled around in her seat. "David, No," she shouted as I broke through the back glass of the camper. My feet hit the ground running. I fled into the woods. I had to get as far away from them as I could. I was insane with thirst. I ran as hard and as fast as I could until I had nothing left in me. I fell to the ground without the strength to go on. The thirst took me. I was gone.

***

I awoke without thirst in cool comfort.

"The child will be born." His liquid smooth voice prompted me to open my eyes. A white marble floor pressed up against my outstretched body. The stone felt exhilaratingly cool against my face.

"For all his meddling, it was I who tipped the balance. Is it so wrong to persuade others? Is it wrong to influence the will of the masses for a greater good?" he said as I stood to my feet. "The destination, that's the important thing to remember. Not the road to get there. We both want the same thing David. Follow him and there will be great suffering, I promise you. I can end all pain, all suffering, David," he added as he paced around beneath the vaulted ceiling. A misty, cool breeze flowed through the wall-less structure. Large columns were the only impediment to the view of a crystal blue sea.

"What do you want from me?" I asked.

"I want your cooperation. I want your partnership. I want to be the Devil's advocate. Forgive me, David. I couldn't help myself," he said with a grin.

"And if I say no?" I asked.

"I'll take the child!" he growled.

***

Agony greeted me when I opened my eyes. I was pretty sure I was going to die right there. I didn't have the strength to get up, let alone hunt some animal to satisfy my thirst. It felt like I was being consumed by fire from the inside. My bones burned like red-hot pokers. I remember wondering if that was what Hell felt like.

It seemed like an eternity passed before I heard them coming. My senses were chaotic so they were on top of me before I saw them. Growling, snarling, sniffing and snorting all around me. *Maybe they'll hurry and kill me,* I remember thinking. And for a moment I truly thought they might.

A pair of massive clawed hands dug deep into my flesh. They felt like daggers of ice lodged in my burning muscle and bone. I was hoisted off the ground and slung over a heavily muscled shoulder. Coarse hair touched my skin and the familiar sweet musky odor filled my nostrils. I was carried for miles before being tossed to the ground. I didn't know where I was. The thirst was everything. Someone took a fist full of my hair and pulled my head up.

"Drink!" Someone demanded.

Precious blood was poured into my mouth. I took hold of the leather pouch from which it poured and drank greedily. My mind and vision cleared quickly.

"Thank you, "I said as the old woman, Mouge, let my hair free from her gnarled grip.

"More trouble than you're worth, I say," she said gruffly and then groaned as she pushed old bent body from the ground beside me. The rich red earth was packed firm and grassless beneath a towering expanse of timber. A large cabin squatted on short legs sat a few yards away.

Three very sturdy, very angry looking young men stood over me. They were undoubtedly my means of arriving at the feet of Mouge. "Get him up," she said as she hobbled toward the cabin. All three grabbed me with unkind hands and hoisted me up and beyond my feet. I caught myself cleanly, having had all me senses return.

"Feeling better are we?" she asked without turning.

"Yes, I am, "I replied. "Thank you, "I added.

Sean, Sam, Sarah, Joshua and the two younger boys, Alex and Luke, all stood on the small porch. They all wore the same grave expression. The three new arrivals, Joshua, Alex and Luke all stared at me through bloodshot, watery eyes. *They hate me*, I thought to myself. I came into their lives and as a result Ann now lay in bed responding to nothing but the pain of her unending thirst. I felt responsible for Ann and for them and I hated being bound by the need to drink. Mouge limped her way up the three wooden stairs to the porch and into the cabin. The children save Sean filed in behind her.

"Are you okay?" Sarah asked as she walked out to me.

"I'm fine now. I had to get away. I went too long. Ann warned me not to wait. She said I had to drink or the thirst would take me, and I would drink. What kind of blood was that?" I asked. "It had a strange taste, "I added.

"Rat poison," she replied.

"Rat blood? I drank rat blood?" I said with obvious disgust.

"No, the blood was her own but rat poison was the only thing around to keep it from coagulating. She was getting ready to go look for you herself when they brought you back. She had already mixed the blood and the poison together in the canteen to carry it with her," she said.

"I don't think she likes me very much, "I said.

"She doesn't like vampires in general. This is all very new for everyone. Mouge has been around a long time. During the time of persecution, when vampires began to slaughter us, many werewolves fled to this region and many more migrated here over the centuries. Mouge's mother was among them. Like many others she settled here and made a family. Mouge's father was native. They accepted werewolves openly. Their legends speak of the Lord of Heaven sending supernatural creatures in times of need. And during that time, many Europeans began to make their way into these lands, bringing disease and wiping out scarce resources. Werewolves were seen as heavens natural response to those problems. Mouge was a child of that era; she was brought up with the tales of the vampires and the destruction they wrought. It's a difficult thing for her to accept. Think about it, David. Ann was there. She was one of them. Give her time. Give everyone time to adjust, including me," she said.

"Is Mouge one of you?" I asked.

"Yes, David. She is," she replied. "That's the way it is with us. It is passed on from parent to child. We are born, we live, love, we die and some of us are long lived while others are not. We can't live forever."

The distant sound of moaning broke the brief silence we shared. I looked behind me and the werewolves who had brought me there had disappeared silently into the forest. When I turned back, Sarah was walking briskly to the cabin. I followed. The mood inside was one of heavy sadness. Tears flowed freely from the little ones gathered around the bed in which Ann continued her tortured slumber. Ann's moans had become much louder and more desperate.

"Why isn't she drinking?" I asked.

"Because if Marcus was wrong, damnation is about to come into the world. Right here in this place." Mouge answered.

"It's time? Already?" I asked.

Just then Ann let out an agonizing cry.

"Everyone out! Out!" Mouge shouted. "You. Boy," she said to Sean.

You keep yourself outside that door and don't let nobody in. You understand?" she asked.

He nodded silently and made his way to the door.

"You two, you stay here. I don't know what's comin'," she warned.

Sarah and I remained inside the room. The old woman carried out the duties of a mid-wife like she had done it a thousand times but her remaining eye was ever wide and taking in every movement, every sound. She was on edge. As she worked I noticed how badly knotted and swollen her joints were. The fingers on her left hand were curled under and locked in place. All except her thumb. Despite her condition she was quite capable. Ann began to labor hard and her cries became loud and sorrowful. Her eyes remained unopened. Tiny beads of bloody sweat began to gather all over her body and turned the white gown and the sheets beneath her to a soft pink. After a few minutes Mouge whispered coarsely, "It's coming."

Ann began to scream as the tiny infant left her body and fell into the waiting hands of the astonished old woman. The soft cry of a baby was suddenly the only sound. The old woman stood up and coddled the child close.

"It's beautiful," she said softly. She handed me the tiny bundled little boy, his eyes, a beautiful and shimmering black, like a star-filled night sky. His hair a wispy white blonde. His tiny, pink fingers and toes were perfect and ten. He looked at me and I knew he saw me. He knew.

"David," The sound of Ann's voice startled me. "David, let me hold him. Please," she said weakly.

"Of course, "I replied and placed him gently on her chest. Her hands left pink prints on his blanket as she drew him close.

"Oh David, He is perfect. I love you," she whispered as she kissed his cheeks. "I don't want to leave him. I'm so cold. David, listen to me. Promise me you will be there for him. Promise me you will protect him," she pleaded.

"I promise, Ann. I promise," I replied. "What should we call him?"

"Eden," she replied.

It was the last sound to escape her lips. She had hemorrhaged. She had lost too much blood during delivery. She was gone. I remember thinking what a strange mix of emotions I felt at that moment. I was over-come with joy to be holding my beautiful, perfect son, and grief stricken again that he would never know his mother. Then there were the children who waited outside with hearts already breaking. How was I going to walk out there and tell them their mother, the woman, the vampire who adopted them, cared for them and most importantly, loved them unconditionally, was dead? It was obvious they loved her in the same manner. They had accepted her for what she was, a beautiful, loving mother who happened to be a vampire. But I didn't have to walk out and tell them.

The door thrust open and the little one, Luke, rushed in already wailing and crying. He begged her not to go over and over. The others joined in his misery. It was the most painful thing I have ever witnessed. Their suffering struck a chord deep inside me. It recalled my own losses and I wished I could take them all in my arms and make it all go away. But I couldn't so there I stood. Holding the very thing that ended her life. I wasn't sure what to expect from them but Alexander backed away from the bedside and became solemn and still. He looked to me and took notice of the bundle I held in my arms and slowly rounded the bed as he wiped his eyes on his sleeves. He stood close and gently pulled the blanket aside to see Eden's face.

"He looks like mom," he said with a trembling voice, choking back another volley of tears.

"Can I hold him?" he asked with tears still leaking from his big brown eyes.

"Of course, "I answered. I placed Eden gently in to the arms of his brother.

"I know she's with God now," he whispered. "But it still hurts so bad."

One by one they stayed their cries and gathered around the watchful infant.

"Mother said he would save us all. Why didn't he save her?" Joshua said bitterly and left the room.

"Joshua!" Sean said as he followed after him. "You have to be there for the young ones and for the baby. It's what mom wanted. You know that. Don't come unglued on me. You're the oldest. They need you, especially Luke. I've always been the screw up. I let her down. I let them down all the time. They look up to you

"She always loved you Sean. No matter what, she always loved you and I love you too, brother, even if you are one of them now. I just wasn't ready to give her up. Not yet," Joshua replied.

"None of us were," Sean replied.

"When are you going to explain all of this? I mean this is crazy. We shouldn't be here. Where is Sonja?" Joshua said.

"I will brother, walk with me," Sean replied.

The screen door of the cabin opened and slammed shut. I liked the sound it made. It reminded me of the time I spent with my grandparents. The slap of a screen door was a common sound that I had forgotten until that moment. But the unfamiliar sound of an infant cooing followed it. Alexander still stood staring down at the tiny infant. He smiled softly as he looked down. Luke stood close at his side with tears still streaking down his cheeks. My heart ached for him. I wanted to make things right. I wanted to take away the pain I knew all too well. It wasn't fair that he had to suffer. There was so much suffering in the world, I thought to myself. I thought of the dreams, I knew, given the choice to take away their pain, I would. But I didn't have that power to exercise. They would have to grieve the loss of their mother. I felt an old bitterness churning in my gut. That night I went out and killed an elk to satisfy my thirst and maybe more.

***

The funeral was makeshift, A simple grave, her body wrapped in white linen. Mouge performed the ceremony. Tears of blood and tears of salt fell. Afterward Mouge asked me to go for a drive with her. I nodded in agreement and passed Eden into the waiting hands of Sarah then climbed into her old diesel pick-up.

"I may only have one eye but I see plenty, and I see far," she said frankly.

"What do you mean?" I asked flatly.

"I mean a lot, that child don't suckle, It ain't taken in a thing. Not one drop of nothin. I don't know what it is but it ain't one of you and it ain't human either. The last time I laid eyes on Marcus he was headin' out to stop you and her from bringin' that child into this world. Now I find out he paid for its life with his own head. I trust his judgment but I don't understand it. I'm hopin' you can help me understand a few things," she said.

"I was sort of hoping the same thing," I replied.

"Now you got questions I can't answer. And some I won't answer but I'm gonna tell ya what ya need to know. But you got to do some answerin' first," she said.

"Alright then, shoot," I replied.

"What do you believe in, David?" she asked.

"What do you mean?" I asked.

You know what I mean. Do you have faith in something?"

"I don't know," I replied. "I used to, a long time ago. But I don't know how to get back."

"They's many, many roads to God, David. It don't matter which one you take. But you'd better take one. Cause something big is comin'. David, that child, it means something. And I had a vision of you. I seen you standin' over that baby, only he was a little boy, all blonde hair and smiles. He was looking up at you. And you was locked arm in arm, face to face with yourself, with another you. You was wrestling with yourself over that boy. You got any idea what that means?" she asked.

"Maybe," I answered.

"What kinda answer is maybe?" she quipped.

"What do you believe in Mouge?" I asked.

"I believe in God and I believe in Heaven. And I believe God made me what I am and put me, and my kind on this earth for a reason. I believe he made you and your kind what you are. And he put you here for a reason. I believe he has a plan for all of us, including that child. But he won't make us follow his plan, David. You have to choose it. And you are gonna have to make a choice. You listen to ole Mouge," she finished.

I didn't respond but I knew she was right. I was struggling with what I knew was right and what I wanted to believe was right.

"What's it like, when you see things? And do you all have visions?" I asked, changing the subject.

"Some do, some do better than others. Marcus, he could see a lot. When he first came, it wasn't so. He was all turned upside down in his head. But he found peace here, peace and quiet. It takes a quiet mind to see far. The young ones see things sometimes but they see mostly nonsense and can't make nothing out of it. Old folks like me, well, we see a lot, both with our eyes and our minds. It's still different from one to another. Take me. I see, how you say it, symbolism. Some people see things like it was happenin' right in front of 'em."

"How 'bout you, David? You been seein' anything?" she prodded.

"Yes, actually, I have. I have had dreams. Strange dreams. In them I see God, and I see the Devil. They talk to me. They call me by name. It's like they are both leading me in the same direction but on different paths," I said.

"Ya See!" she exclaimed as she hit the horn with the palm of her hand. "See, David? Like I told you. Get on a path to God. The devil will trick you, David. He will make you think it's the right way but it ain't. Don't you get fooled, David," she warned.

"Sarah says your mother was driven here by vampires a long time ago."

"She was," she answered.

"The captain of that ship said that there are a lot of minds to change," I added.

"They are," she replied.

"What changed yours?" I asked.

"She loved that baby. You could feel it fill the room. Love ain't never of the Devil, David. Can't be. That's what changed my mind. That poor girl suffered plenty but when she opened them eyes they was full of nothing but happiness. That's what changed my mind. Them other boys, they loved her too. What's gonna become of them?"

"I don't know," I replied.

"That boy, Sean, he come to Marcus. He wanted to know the truth of things. Marcus told him all about everything. He made up his mind to be one of us. Them other boys, they might do the same. They'd be happy here," she said.

"Maybe, "I replied. "I don't know."

"Well, I know they gonna need somebody," she replied. "Sarah, she gonna need somebody too," she added.

"Where are we going?" I asked, changing the subject.

We had traveled down the now dry and dusty road for several miles. There wasn't a cloud in the sky and the sun was like rich yellow yolk in the sky above us.

"People got to eat. I got to go to town," she answered. "And sides that I'm old and I needed someone to carry the groceries for me," she added with a grin, which all but closed her remaining eye. The dirt road turned on to a narrow paved one then two a two-lane road, which led to the town square. It was mid-day and the small town was milling with townspeople. Small shops lined that the intersecting streets of the square like something from a Norman Rockwell. But as we neared the center of town I noticed that the pedestrians on the streets stopped and stared as we passed. All eyes fell on us as we passed. We parked in front of a row of storefronts, which lined the west most side of town, along the coast of the island.

"Well, don't just sit there," Mouge said, climbing out of the pick-up.

I opened my door and as I did I looked around and couldn't help but notice that everyone in town had ceased their daily errands and activities and stood silently observing the two of us, cars came to a stop in the road. Pedestrians rounded corners and halted in their tracks on the sidewalks. Silence fell over the town. The hair on the back of my neck stood up. I sensed danger all around us.

"Mouge, what's going on?" I asked.

"Well now, they all gonna find out one way or another. Might as well be this way. Come on," she said, stepping up onto the sidewalk.

"Stay close to ole Mouge," she said, motioning me close.

A woman and her child stood several yards down to our left. Both the woman and the child wore the same menacing expression. They reminded me of that look an old scared dog gave just before it bit you. She led us through the door of the shop. A bell jingled on a string as we entered. An old man behind an old wooden counter smiled warmly for a moment before his face went slack and his warm eyes went cold.

"What in the hell is that doing here? You get out of here!" he shouted as he pointed an old bony finger at me.

Just then an old woman appeared from the back of the store.

"George, what's all the shouting about?" she asked as she hurried to his side.

She gasped and covered her mouth with her feeble hands and stared at me with eyes wide with fear. She quickly clutched the arm of the old man as if she needed his protection. Mouge stopped and turned sideways to me, she leaned over and looked passed me then turned back to the old man.

"You feelin' okay, George? I don't see nothing." she said.

"Where did he come from? Why is he here?!" The old woman hissed.

"Oh, him?" Mouge asked, gesturing to me.

"Mouge what the hell do you think you are doing?! You know exactly what he is. How and why is he here?" The old man demanded.

A small crowd had gathered outside the doors of the shop and alarms were now going off inside my head.

"I swear, George. I don't know why I keep comin' here. Prices go up and up and your hospitality ain't much anymore," she said as she began taking items from the shelf and placing them in a small basket she had carried in from the truck.

"I'm warning you!" he said as he lifted a shotgun from beneath the counter and aimed it in our general direction. "Get him outta here!" he demanded.

"Now what you gonna do with that? You gonna shoot 'im? Won't do no good, you know that. Or you gonna shoot me? Probably ain't even loaded," she said.

Immediately he raised the gun toward the ceiling and pulled the trigger. A shot thundered from the barrel and bits of the ceiling fell to the floor. I hated guns, God I hated guns. I was pretty sure I had nothing to fear from them anymore but I still hated them. Mouge laughed out loud and shook her head from side to side.

"You old fool. Now you got to fix that roof," she said as she continued to fill her basket.

"Last chance, Mouge," he said as he pointed the gun directly at her. "I don't know what you're meanin' by bringin' that thing into this town but you got 'til the count of three to get him outta here," he said with absolute conviction. "One, Two, Th..."

He had just begun to utter the word when Mouge was on him. She moved like lightning. She ripped the gun from his hands with dagger-like claws clamped around the barrel. She let out an earth-shaking roar and with her one remaining, yellow eye she surveyed the two closely. Both were obviously terrified and pressed themselves hard against the wall. With the agility of an Olympic gymnast she leapt off the counter and landed effortlessly at the front door of the store. Another deafening roar erupted from her throat.

Her teeth were massive and jagged and silver hair streaked her muscled frame. The crowd at the door quickly backed away. She pushed herself up from all fours and before she was completely upright she became the old bent Mouge again.

"Do you got any of those bags of liquorish? We got young ones out to the cabin."

"Damn you, Mouge!" he said and they both disappeared into the back.

"Some people ain't got no manners," she said. "Just put it on my tab," she shouted over her shoulder as she handed the basket to me.

"I don't suppose you need nothing," she said with a mischievous grin before heading for the door.

I followed close behind her as she walked out onto the sidewalk. The crowd had grown larger but had backed away several yards in all directions. I put the groceries into the bed of the truck and was about to get in when a sheriffs car pulled in next to us.

"Hold it right there!" A round faced portly man in uniform shouted with his hand covering the gun on his hip.

More guns, I thought to myself.

He walked around the front of the truck side-stepped as he went, with his eyes locked onto me until he reached the driver's side, where Mouge sat patiently.

"Sheriff," she nodded.

"Mouge, have you lost your damn mind. What is goin' on here?" he demanded.

"Shoppin'," she said with a smile.

"Shoppin'?" he repeated.

"Shoppin'," she said again.

"Well, you care to explain why you have a gall darn vampire sitting in the cab of your truck?"

"I have a vampire in the cab of my truck?" she asked coyly.

"Now Mouge I'm not playin' with you," he cautioned.

"And I really don't got time to play with you neither. Got milk in the back," she said as she started the truck and put it in gear. The sheriff reached in and put his hand on the steering wheel as if to stop her from backing out.

"Yes, I got me a vampire in the cab of my truck. I got me a vampire baby at my cabin. I got me a dead vampire buried in my back yard. They all here cause Marcus sent 'em here. Now it's up to me to keep 'em safe. You got that sheriff? Now you get that hand outta my truck for you draw back a nub," she warned.

The sheriff slowly pulled his hand back out of the truck.

"Now you go on and you tell everybody what I got out to the cabin. And you tell everybody Marcus done sent 'em to me and you tell everybody that Old Mouge be the one to come to if they got something to say," she said as she threw truck into reverse and backed out into the street.

"Bye now sheriff," she called to him and waved as we sped out of town.

"Now that ought to get things goin," she said with a smile.

We drove the dusty roads back to the cabin without a word. I was lost in thought and I think Mouge was as well. The island was her home. It was where she had lived her entire life. She knew these people intimately and she was risking alienating herself from them for us. I liked her a lot. *She reminds me of my grandma.* I thought to myself, glancing over at her.

"I ain't got no grandbabies. Ain't got no children," she said.

"Did you hear what I was thinking?" I asked.

"No, I just seen a picture come into my mind of you and an old woman, looked like me. And you was a little feller, all smiles and no front teeth. Just made me think about not havin' none," she said.

"You remind me of my grandma, a lot," I said.

"How's that?" she asked.

"She was spunky, like you. She wasn't afraid of anything," I answered.

"Oh I'm afraid of plenty, David," she replied.

"What are you afraid of, Mouge?" I asked.

"I'm afraid of you. I'm afraid for you. I'm afraid of what might happen to these folks here. I'm afraid of what it might mean to the world, havin' that little baby in it. I'm afraid others of your kind might find you here and bring death and destruction with 'em. I'm afraid of many things," she replied.

"What about you, boy? What you afraid of?" she continued.

"I don't know Mouge. I'm afraid of losing the ones I love."

"Hmm. Nothin' is forever, David. We all gonna leave this world someday, somehow. If we don't, this ole world will quit us one day. You can't stop things that ain't under your control. People got to be free to do as they will," she added.

"You hear me?" she prodded.

"Yes, I hear you."

"Good. Now we best get ready for company," she said as we pulled up to the cabin.

Sarah came out to meet us.

"Where have you been?" Sarah asked as she walked to the truck.

She was obviously worried. I wasn't glad she was worried but it was nice to know she cared.

"We went into town, to the grocery store," I replied.

"You took him into town? Mouge are you crazy?" she asked with surprise in her voice.

"Why does everybody got to be askin' me if I'm crazy all the time? Startin' to get on my nerves. Ain't nothing on this island Mouge can't handle. Besides, didn't nothing happen. But we gonna be having guests tonight." Mouge replied.

"Who?" Sarah asked with concern.

"Oh I suspect the sheriff and maybe a few others. I suspect Roland'll be comin' too," she replied.

"Mouge what have you done?" she pleaded.

"Mouge ain't done nothing. People on this island gonna find out soon enough. All I done was get things movin'. People seen him, people know they here, and now they know Mouge is the one to come to," Mouge replied.

"Who is Roland?" I asked.

"He's an elder, like Marcus and Mouge," Sarah replied.

"Now I ain't no elder no more. I'm just plain old now," Mouge broke in. "All Roland cares about is money, money, money. That's all he thinks about. He ain't no elder neither. Dollar signs is god now. Our ways don't mean nothing to him no more. All he gonna wanna know is how this is gonna affect the price of tea in china. We ain't got no leader no more. With Marcus dead, our people gonna divide, gonna be lost. Roland ain't the man for the job. And I'm too old, just too old. And besides that, I'm crazy," she finished as she limped toward the cabin.

"David, bring them groceries!" she called back to me.

"David, this is serious. Roland is not like Marcus. He is a man of the new world and Mouge is right, he cares a lot about money but that's his place. He manages everything. He is responsible for us all. He sees to it that we all have jobs, money, land, security. He manages our entire financial empire, the shipping, real estate, manufacturing, the stock market, everything. He's a powerful, hard man. But I think he still cares for our ways. And when he finds out about you, Eden and the others he will come," she said.

"What should we do?" I asked

"What you should do is bring them groceries in!" Mouge shouted from the door.

"Age has not diminished your hearing," Sarah whispered.

"Nope." Mouge replied, then let the screen door slam.

"Is she always like that?" I asked.

"For as long as I have known her," Sarah replied.

"What did she mean by not being an elder anymore?" I asked.

"Elders are our leaders, they are appointed for life. Mouge was once the appointed Elder for this part of our world she was considered strong, respected and wise in a time before great ships and cars and airplanes. It was a much harsher existence back then and our kind withdrew from the outside world. We feared anyone who was not of our own. We lived off the land and took care of one another. She was young and beautiful then. I have heard the stories of how she captivated the heart of any man who laid eyes on her. But she had no time for love or family. She was married to our people as a whole."

"She devoted herself to governing this region our then fragile kingdom. Roland was Elder to the Northland. He governed from what is now Alaska, across the sea and into Russia. Life was hard but it was peaceful. But the world grew around us and in time, humans came into our world. The first outsider to come into the village that once stood on this island was a man by the name of Charles Everheart. He simply strode right into the middle of everything. Seeing a white man was no surprise. After all most of our ancestors had fled from Europe as Mouge's mother had."

"It was his scent that drove everyone wild. He'd have been killed had Mouge not saved him. She came between him and her own kind. Outrage spread like wildfire and news soon reached Roland's ears. He came to the island immediately to see for himself the man that Mouge had stood against her own people to spare. But like I said Mouge stole many hearts and Charles Everheart was no exception. And he had captured hers as well. They fell in love the moment their eyes met. That's why she saved him. She loved him. Roland was furious and demanded that Mouge hand her lover over to him. She refused. And the two of them fought. Mouge had been very careful not to allow Charles to see the nature of what we really are. But Roland in his rage transformed himself into his werewolf form while Charles looked on in horror."

146

"Mouge had no choice but to defend herself. She too shifted into wolf form and the two leaders fought an epic battle right here in this very spot. Mouge defeated Roland but she lost her eye. Not only that, she lost Charles. They say he went mad, Mouge won't talk about it but they say she kept him here for a time. She tried to calm him, reason with him. She tried to persuade him to become one of us but Roland's actions had forever changed him. Mouge was heartbroken. She had to let him go. She followed him well beyond the borders of our world but eventually she had to watch him disappear from sight, not knowing if he lived or died."

"They say she was never the same. Soon after she stepped down as Elder but she has never forgiven Roland. He has, over the years tried to make amends but Mouge won't have it. She says not forgiving Roland will be the one thing God will hold her accountable for. Some wounds just don't heal I suppose," she said.

"No I guess they don't, "I replied.

"It's an awful thing to love someone and have to give them up," she said.

"I didn't know, Sarah," I replied.

Tears welled up in the lids of her eyes. "I never stopped loving you, David. Never," she continued. "I have cried a thousand nights. I have wanted to come to you so many times. There were moments that I didn't care what Sonja would do to me. I felt it couldn't be any worse than the life I was living. I still love you, David. And I am terrified that you will never love me again and even more afraid that you will love me and I'll lose you again. David, please say something," she pleaded.

The heart that rested now silently in my chest burned with the sweetest pain. Oh how I loved her. I had dreamed of hearing those words over and over. I closed my eyes and the words erupted from my very heart and from my heart to my lips to Gods ears.

"Thank you God for bringing her back to me!" I whispered with eyes still closed; "I am humble and broken before you. Do with me what you will I am your vessel," I said choking back tears.

I opened my vampire eyes and took in the wonder and beauty that God had returned to me.

"I love you with everything I am. I don't ever want to let you go."

She wiped the blood from my cheeks with her gentle hands and whispered, "You won't have to. I am yours in this life and the next, David Cross," she whispered.

I took her in my arms but with delicate care. "You won't hurt me, David," she said gazing deep into my eyes.

I pulled her tight against me with as much strength as I dared. A whispered moan escaped her lips as she returned my embrace, matching my vampire strength if not more. I could have died in that moment with no regrets. But I didn't and the moment was cut short by the sound of the screen door opening.

"If you done moonin', Sarah, get on in here. We got a special dinner to make for company t'nite," she grinned.

"Mouge, I know that look. What are you up to?" Sarah asked.

"I ain't up to nothing, but Roland ain't never said no to a meal in his life. I'm just gonna cook something special for him. And you gonna give it to him," she said.

"Why me?" Sarah asked incredulously.

"Cause he ain't gonna say no to you neither," she replied.

"Mouge, please don't start a fight," Sara said.

"Mouge ain't startin' nothing. Don't you worry 'bout nothing. Ole Mouge knows what she is doin', now git on in here and help. David you git on in here and tend to that baby. I don't know what kinda tendin' it might need but them youngins ain't put it down not one time."

"I guess we'd better get in there, I've seen her mad," I said with a grin.

"Mouge, what happened in town?" Sarah asked with concern.

"Now there you go again, thinking old Mouge lost her mind. Well I ain't lost all of it, now go!" she ordered.

We hastily obeyed and once inside we found the boys hovering around. Young Alex, who had Eden cradled in his loving arms, was pleading with him to drink. Alex had pricked his finger and was trying desperately to encourage the silent infant to drink.

"May I?" I asked with outstretched hands. Alex looked up at me with through two giant orbs with lakes of tears threatening to crest.

"Why won't he eat?" he sobbed. "What's wrong with him?" he pleaded. "He's all I have left of Mom. He has to be okay," he said cupping his face in his hands to hide the tears that flowed in rivulets down his ruddy cheeks.

My heart ached for him, and for all the boys. Ann had been the only mother they had known. She had not given birth to them. She wasn't even human but she was without a doubt the finest mother they could have had. I felt a welling guilt for being a part of her demise but they held no contempt for me, or for the child she gave her life to bring into the world. I marveled at their grace, which they clearly inherited from their mother. I held Eden gently in my arms. His eyes fixed on mine and I felt no distress. He wanted for nothing. He was warm and soft and the soft sweet scent of a baby wafted into my nasal passages.

"What are you, little guy?" I whispered.

"Maybe he needs a doctor, he doesn't eat or drink or anything. Maybe he's sick," Luke blurted out.

"Sarah, what do you see? Anything?" I asked.

"May I hold him?" she asked not of me but of the children.

"Yes," Joshua answered.

Sarah took him from my arms with care and ease. She held him close and closed her eyes. Her brow furrowed and her eyes squinted in concentration. After a moment, a slight tilt of her head hinted that she might have caught some image or some tiny clue.

"I feel nothing but well-being, a deep peace and calm," she said opening her eyes.

"What do you think?" I asked.

"I don't know but David, he is heavier than he was. I think he has grown already. Look at him," she said as she unwrapped him. She was right.

"He looks weeks old David. I don't understand it but he is growing," she said.

"Mouge, can you come here?" she called to the kitchen.

Mouge appeared quickly through the doorway of the kitchen still holding a bowl in her bent arthritic hand.

"Look at this," Sarah said to her.

Mouge limped across the room and peered intently at Eden.

"Sarah, girl, that baby ain't nussed or wet the first time and still grows like a weed. This ain't no baby. Ain't no baby like I ever seen. It ain't no vampire neither. This child is special. This child be something real special. This child be a gift from God," she said as she took Eden into her arms, the white mixing bowl still hanging from her crooked fingers.

She eyed Eden closely.

"Do you see anything, Mouge?" Sara asked.

"Twice I have felt something from him, something unique," she continued. "Hmm, Mouge don't see nothing more than a beautiful child," she said with a smile. "Mouge don't know what part you got to play in this big world but Mouge gonna make sure you get to play it," she said to Eden and kissed him on the forehead.

She continued to look into his large, dark eyes. Motionless, she stood. The moment grew, concern mounted.

"Mouge, are you okay?" Sarah asked.

Mouge didn't respond. Her eyes remained fixed on Eden.

"Mouge" Sarah said again.

I reached out to touch her but before my hand reached her shoulder she gasped and took in a deep breath, breaking her gaze at Eden. The mixing bowl, which had she had held with her crooked fingers, fell to the floor and shattered.

"Mouge! What's wrong?" Sarah shouted.

The children who had been silently observing, all sprang to their feet.

"Mouge, what is it?" Sarah said with alarm.

"Take him," she gasped as she handed him to the children who had gathered close. Luke who had crowded the closest took him from her quickly and Mouge rushed from the room. Sarah and I followed her into the kitchen where she stood at the sink with her back to us.

"What happened in there, Mouge?" I asked.

She did not answer.

"Mouge, are you alright? Did you see something?" Sarah asked.

The old woman turned around slowly, she caressed her left hand with her right, as she turned.

"Mouge saw something. But don't know what," she answered. "But that ain't all," she added. She held up her left hand and before us and splayed her now straight and limber fingers.

"No bigger than that little Luke in there I was, my papaw told me 'bout them days when the Lord of Heaven sent powerful creatures to this earth. Lord looked down and seen that the world of man was in trouble, more than once. And sent down what was needed to set it right. There's been many things walkin' round in man flesh, like me and you. But I don't know of nothing like that child," she said.

Mouge walked passed us and back to the living room with a now even gait. Her limp was completely absent. She went to Luke who was still holding Eden. She knelt close and laid her newly restored hand on Eden's tiny chest.

"Thank you, child." she said softly.

Sean, who had been almost silent since Ann's passing, spoke up.

"What was it, what's going on? Your hand, it's...it's not. Did Eden do that?" he asked. "Did he?" he asked again without allowing time for her to answer.

"If he can do that, why didn't he save his own mother?" he shouted.

Mouge rose to her full height and turned to Sean. "Now you listen to Mouge and you listen good. That sweet girl left this world with nothin' but love in her heart, love for you and these other boys. She done what she done outta love, they ain't no better cause than that. Now don't you raise that voice in this house no more. I know you hurtin', but don't you go askin' why things got to be they way they is. They just is. And what would your mama want you to be doin'? Blamin'? Holdin' fault? Or would she want you to be lovin' something she gave her life for? Now you think about that." Mouge said as she finished with an emphatic nod, re-examined her unbent fingers and returned to the kitchen.

"Are you okay, Sean?" I asked.

"She's right," he answered. "It just hurts."

"Come on, let's go see her," Sara said putting her arm around Sean's shoulders.

The pair walked out the door with heads hung in a shared silence. The remaining children gathered around Eden with new enthusiasm and curiosity. Even Joshua seemed to be in awe of him. I didn't know what he was or how he was thriving without eating or drinking but he was beautiful and had just displayed an amazing gift without a sound. Frequently his large endless gaze sought me out as if he needed to communicate something to me but without the ability to read minds and his inability to speak left us cut off from one another.

"We gonna have company real soon," Mouge said, appearing in the doorway. "Mouge needs some help in here," she added, motioning for me to come with her.

Once in the kitchen she quickly put me to work, mixing and stirring. She prepared a wonderful meal fit for a king and large enough for an army. She somehow managed to get everything done at once and just in time. She was setting the table when we all heard a car, or cars pulling up. We all rushed to the door but Mouge was out on the porch first.

Three dark Escalades pulled up in front of the cabin. It was getting dark and it had just started raining. Sean and Sarah rounded the porch and climbed to the stairs to join us, looking over their shoulders at the convoy as they did. Windshield wipers swiped away the rain from the blackened windows of the trucks. But that and the billowing steam from the exhaust were the only movements.

"Come on outta there Roland," Mouge shouted. "I won't bite, this time," she said with a grin.

The engines all turned off at once and then passenger door of the lead vehicle opened slowly. A large black boot struck the ground. Followed by another, then a large pale hand grasped the top of the opened door. A tall, overweight, older man hauled himself up from seat. He was unimpressive at first sight. He had the look of an unhealthy man and his close-set eyes made him look dim and shifty. His form managed to make his six hundred dollar suit look bad and he moved like a giant sloth, as if each movement took considerable effort. He stopped his forward movement and searched the group of us until his beady eyes found mine. He stood still and glared hard at me as if he had read my thoughts and he couldn't manage to walk and look for me at the same time. After a moment he began to lumber towards us again.

"Close enough!" Mouge shouted.

He halted a few yards from the porch.

"Who you foolin'? Not me," Mouge said slyly. "What you doin' here, Roland? And who you got with you?"

Roland looked over his shoulder at the parked SUV's. A group of sturdy men and one portly Sheriff emerged.

"Evenin', Sheriff," Mouge waved with her former bad hand.

The movement did not go un-noticed by Roland. I saw his tiny black eyes fix on it quickly. He was not as dim as he appeared, I thought to myself. Again his eyes shifted to me.

"Hand him over Mouge," Roland demanded.

His voice was flat and casual. It was not very threatening. It seemed more of a suggestion.

"Now you know that ain't gonna happen. You ain't brought enough help," Mouge replied.

"Looks to me like I have plenty of help," he said as he motioned for his men to approach.

As soon as he did Mouge let out a sharp whistle and three massive wolves stepped from the forest into the clearing.

"You met by nephews, Roland?" she asked. But before he could respond she continued, "Oh but you not met this young man," she said pointing to the wolf on the right.

The wolves advanced closer and as they did they shifted into human form.

"This young man be Sam. He a fine young man."

"Sam!" Sean shouted as he jumped the rail and ran to Sam. He slammed into him with a hearty hug and a huge smile on both their faces.

"You made the change!" Sean shouted.

The two youths reveled in their new brotherhood for a moment before turning to face Roland's men. Now they were four strong.

"Now have you met this young thing? This be Sarah, she be a fine young woman. Now let ole Mouge think. That makes six countin' me, don't it? Now if I had to bet, if you boys come to my place and me all alone, good money be that Mouge all by her lonesome would cover this ground with you all's insides. Now you got two choices. Mouge can give you to the count of three to get back in your fancy car and get off this land or you respect that you on Mouge's land."

"You show respect to me and mine and you come in Mouge's house as my guest and take my hospitality. You been trying to set things right a long time. Now be your chance," Mouge said.

Roland blew the rain from his lips. He surveyed the scene, looking at the four werewolves to his left, to Mouge and finally to his men. He motioned for them to get back in the cars. They quickly jumped back in the cars and retreated back down the road.

"Good!" Mouge said with a smile. "Come in outta that rain."

He lumbered to the steps of the porch and as he drew closer I noticed he was older than he had appeared at a distance. Not quite as old as Mouge but he didn't possess the same vitality she possessed. This man was not well. A third time he glared at me as if hearing my every thought. I didn't care if he did. I sensed no physical danger from him. But I also had the feeling there was more to him than met the eye. He stalked passed me and into the house. His very presence filled the house with discomfort.

"Come, warm by the fire," Mouge said as she rekindled a small smoldering fire in the fireplace.

She kept a fire at night in the cabin. Even in midsummer on the island the temperature dropped dramatically at night. And the clouds and rain added to the chill. He walked slowly with wide heavy steps over to the fireplace and turned his back to the hearth, facing the room and all of us. His small eyes scanned the room. Searching each one of us. A flash of something crossed his face as he focused his eyes on Eden. But he quickly regained his composure.

"We don't allow outsiders here, you should know that. What if some tourist had seen your display in town? You put us all at risk. Their being here puts us all at risk," he said.

"Roland, we gonna sit, break bread and then we talk. If Mouge got apologies' to make then she make 'em'," Mouge replied.

"You apologize to me?" Roland asked incredulously.

"Watch that tone in this house, you heard right," she replied.

"You children go finish settin' the table," Mouge said as she walked to the front door. She opened the door and called to the young men who still stood guard outside.

"You boys come up here outta the rain. Don't you let nobody come near. You keep watch. Sarah gonna bring you a plate of good cookin'," she said.

"Thanks Aunt Mouge," one of the brawny young men said as he kissed her on the cheek.

Mouge closed the door and called everyone to the table. No one moved until Roland saw that we were unwilling to leave the living room until he had. He moved in slow fashion to the dining room table.

"Now you set here, at the head of the table," Mouge said pulling out the chair for him.

We all took our seats around the table and Mouge set about filling plates and pouring drinks, obviously leaving my plate empty.

"Your kind doesn't eat. Do they?" Roland asked with a lack of kindness.

"Now Roland you fill that mouth and talk later," Mouge said.

"I was just going to say that it's a shame. Everyone knows what a good cook you are," Roland replied.

Eating was the only thing he did quickly. He shoveled spoonful after spoonful into his mouth. Not halting for a second as he commented on how good it was and how he hadn't had a home cooked meal in ages. He emptied several plates before pushing himself back from the table.

"Mouge I never would have dreamed I'd be sitting in your house, enjoying a meal like this. We should have buried the hatchet eons ago."

"Mouge is old and set in her ways," she replied.

"I'm not young anymore either and time hasn't been too kind to me," he replied. "But I see you seem to be getting around nicely. What's your secret?" he asked.

"Some people do got secrets but Mouge ain't got none," she replied. "Now hold on, I do got a secret. I don't tell nobody the recipe to apple pie."

"Did you save room for desert? I could get you a slice of pie," Sarah said right on cue.

Roland's eyes lingered a little too long on Sarah before he answered yes. She could probably have offered to cut off his head and he'd have answered the same. I tried to keep my thoughts from being so readily available to him but I couldn't help but wonder how he managed to obtain any sort of control or power. But his ability to see the minds of others, or at least mine was very keen.

"You don't like me very much do you?" he said to me.

"No, I don't think I do," I replied.

He didn't respond he just sat back and laced his fingers across his round belly. Mouge watched carefully. Sarah returned with a slice of steaming hot apple pie.

"It's fresh from the oven," she said with a smile.

He took the plate from her while purposefully overlapping his hands onto her hers as he took it. The move made me angry.

"Aren't you going to have some?" he asked Sarah.

"Yes, I think I will," she replied and returned to the kitchen.

"Excuse us," Joshua said.

And the children stood from the table and made their way back to the living room having hardly touched their meals. Roland paid them little attention as he set about devouring the pie.

"Mouge, this pie is delicious," he said. "I think this is the best...I think this is the best...the best...uh...I uh... What? Uh," he shook his head trying to clear his mind but it was no use. He was rapidly slipping into a stupor.

"Ain't no good keeping secrets, Roland. Ain't no good at all. Mouge puts just a little Tansy flower, specially prepared, in that apple pie, that's my secret ingredient just for you," Mouge said.

"Mouge you didn't, it will kill him," Sarah said rushing from the kitchen.

"Naw, not in that dose it won't. But now ole Mouge can see that his secrets comin' clear," Mouge said as she leaned in close to him. Roland struggled against the drug to keep his mind closed. "Now what has you been up to?" she asked, not expecting an answer from his lips but rather from his mind.

Roland jolted in the chair as if a nerve had been struck. Mouges one eye flashed wide with panic. She sprang from the table and burst through the front door, shifting into wolf form and landing on all fours in a defensive posture. She snarled and growled in every direction at the empty night. She stood to her feet and let out a long deafening howl. Her nephews and Sam and Sean quickly changed their forms. Sarah shifted seconds later as if cued by the mournful howl.

"What's happening?" I shouted.

Mouge ended her haunting call. Dozens of howls echoed in the forest from all around us. She turned and looked at me with her piercing yellow eye.

"Vampires," she said in a chilling, guttural voice.

"Eden," I said aloud and ran to the living room.

The children were already standing at alarm with Luke clutching Eden close to his chest.

"What's going on?" Joshua demanded with false bravado in his voice. They were all very frightened.

"They've come for Eden," I said.

"Who? Who has come?" Alex asked.

"Sonja," I answered.

"She can't have him." Luke shouted.

"It's going to be okay," I assured him.

"Where is Sean?" Joshua asked.

"He's with Mouge and Sarah," I replied. Joshua bolted from the room. "Joshua, wait," I called to him but he pressed on.

"Kids come on, come into the dining room. Stay together," I instructed.

They followed me into the dining room obediently and huddled at the other end of the room as far from Roland as they could. I could hear Joshua arguing with Sean who had shifted back to human form for the benefit of his brother.

"You don't know that," I heard him say to Sean.

"What has she ever done to us?" Joshua demanded, speaking of Sonja.

There was a brief commotion and then Joshua came falling back through the door with Sam half in wolf form on top of him.

"She killed me Mum, Joshua. Ain't that enough?" he roared, slamming him to the ground and knocking over the table

"Get off of me!" Joshua shouted.

"Let him go Sam," Sean said following them through the door.

"Sam, let him go," I said.

"Right. Okay," Sam responded with his human mouth but his wolf eyes still flashed with anger. He had just begun to push himself from the ground to release the obviously shaken Joshua when with his right hand, Joshua grasped a knife, which had fallen to the floor and plunged it deep into Sam's leg. He let out a roar and in an instant his human features had vanished and nothing but werewolf remained. Before anyone could move he had viciously bitten Joshua on the neck. Blood sprayed from the wound.

"Now you can see with your own eyes!" Sam growled.

I hadn't fed in quite some time and though I could feel myself becoming stronger and able to resist the urge to feed a little more each day, the sight of the blood sent my mind reeling. Sarah rushed to his side while screaming at Sam to get out of her way. The scene slowed and their voices seemed miles away and echoed in my head. The world was in chaos. I felt the waves of heat lapping at my face. The cool panic crept up my spine. I was being taken by the need to drink. I had to go.

"He didn't ask for it, what have you done?" I heard Sarah shout at Sam from some distant place.

I was moving but I didn't know to where. I was vaguely aware of the wind in my face and of the burning inside me as my blood starved muscles spirited me away from the cabin. Some hidden, primal part of my mind had taken over and was now driving me into the night for the singular purpose of obtaining blood, a lot of it. The forest was ripe with the smell of it. Nocturnal creatures scampered away from my rapid approach, their tiny hearts resounding in my head. But they were of no consequence. I wanted more.

Though I didn't realize it on a conscious level, I was closing in on the small town nearby with deadly desires. But she was faster than I was. She overtook me just in sight of the dim street-lights of town. She hit me hard from behind. The momentum of our bodies drove my face and shoulders into the earth, tearing a shallow but lengthy rip in the earth. Her jaws locked firmly but forgivingly around my neck. Her giant claws pressed hard against my resistant flesh.

"I can't let you do this," she said in a gravelly but feminine voice as she released her bite. "I love you but I can't let you hurt these people," she said as her voice cleared to the familiar velvet sound of Sarah's voice.

The feel of her claws replaced by the sensation of her delicate hands against skin. I was still a wild animal. Still full of the primal desire to drink, and now a new desire competed for dominance. The scent of her, the beating of her heart, it was as if her entire body pulsed and throbbed against my back with each contraction of her heart. I turned beneath her, her body still hot from the chase, steamed in the cool night air and burned my flesh. The mix of thirst and want was overwhelming. She bent to kiss my hard, cold lips and I could smell her rich blood. I could see it fill the capillaries in her blushing cheeks. Her kiss was like liquid fire. My fingers dug into the earth like anchors at the ends of my outstretched arms.

"Drink," she whispered as she bared her neck to me and pressed her body into mine.

There was no question. There was no argument. I had to have her, all of her.

***

"I do hope you understand. I couldn't leave anything to chance," he said with charm dripping from his tongue like liquor from a brush.

"I had so hoped the scales would tip in my favor without having to resort to all this violence but you seemed to be leaning in the other direction and I simply could not let that happen."

We were in the forest. It felt very much like the woods that surrounded the cabin. But I was alone with him. Sarah was nowhere in sight.

"Where is she? Where is Sarah?" I demanded.

"Oh don't get yourself so worked up, David," he said. "I have no interest in her. I only want the child," he added.

As he spoke I noticed the faint scent of smoke lingering around my nostrils. I inhaled deeply and the thick scent of burning wood filled my lungs.

"What have you done?" I said angrily.

"I have done nothing. I have but only my influence at my disposal in your world. But what's done is done. I have much to attend to and for the moment I have no need of you. Goodbye my beautiful David," he said wistfully.

Chapter Eight

The thief cometh not, but for to steal, and to kill, and to destroy: I am come that they might have life, and that they might have [it] more abundantly
John 10:10

The morning dew was cold against my skin. Sarah lay motionless in my arms. Our clothing was torn and covered in still wet blood. For a moment I feared she was dead but I saw the faintest rise in her chest.

"Sarah, Sarah," I whispered.

She groaned and opened her eyes slowly. "I'm weak," she whispered.

"Sarah, something has happened," I said to her.

"I smell smoke," she said sleepily.

"I do too," I answered.

"We have to get back, now."

"Come on, I'll carry you, "I said as I lifted her easily in my arms. "Did I hurt you?"

"Did I hurt you?" she replied with a faint smile.

"No, you didn't," I answered with a smile. "Ready?"

"Yes," she replied and I ran in the direction of the cabin as quickly as I dared while carrying her.

The smell of burnt wood thickened as we neared the clearing. I inhaled frequently to determine if it did. A great fear welled up inside me the closer we got to the cabin. I wondered if my dreams were more than dreams. I wondered if I had truly been visited by the Devil and if so, where was the old man? Why hadn't he come to me in my dreams lately?

We broke through the line of trees and my worst fears didn't compare to the sight in front of us. The cabin had been reduced to nothing more than a pit of smoldering black ash. Bodies lay scattered on the ground, covered in blood and dirt. Mouge's nephews, Roland's men, the sheriff, all dead. Mouge alone survived.

"Put me down," Sarah said.

She stumbled for a moment like a new born fawn but the sight of Mouge's body lying on the ground filled her with panic and adrenaline.

"Mouge!" she screamed.

We ran to her. She lay face down in the dirt. It was clear her arm was dislocated and she had lost a lot of blood from wounds on her back but she was alive.

"Mouge are you alright? Oh my God, Mouge. What happened? Where are the children? Where is Eden?" I asked with tremendous fear in my voice.

"Mouge will be alright. But they took 'em. We tried to stop em but they come in like ghosts and out like demons. These boys, they ain't had no fight. They ain't never known nothing but a good life. They wasn't ready for this. But they fought to the last. They all dead. And Mouge should be dead too. That old one, she be stronger than old Mouge. They all come at me. They was five, six, maybe more. My nephews' lyin' dead over there, they saved Mouge. They get them off Mouge, all but the dark one. She come to kill ole Mouge. Mouge is old but fierce. The beast in Mouge is strong but was no good. She break bone and tear flesh 'til Mouge be weak and got no fight. Somethin' spook her. She run away without killin' Mouge. She leave Mouge here to cry over the dead. They took them boys and that baby. All but that Joshua. He done been changed and run off. That Sean run after him. They ain't never come back. Ain't nobody left. And Roland, he burned up in my house. Sorry bastard done it to himself. He brung 'em here. Mouge seen it in his mind. He done it for the promise of money and power. He was no good no more. He got to answer to God now. Not to ole Mouge. You two got to find them lost boys. You got to find 'em and go get them children back. That baby got gifts, gifts from God. Ain't no telling what those devils gonna do to, or with that child. You got to stop em. You gots to," she said.

She was exhausted, bloody and broken. We were surrounded by death and destruction. The smell of blood and smoke assaulted my heightened sense. I tried to tell myself to stay calm. She valued Eden. She wouldn't harm him. And the other children were taken to use as pawns no doubt. I closed my eyes and tried to stave off the intense anger building inside me.

"David, we'll get them back. We'll find them," Sarah whispered as she held Mouge's battle torn body in her arms.

Mouge began to weep, she cried for the loss of her loved ones. She even cried for the death of Roland and cried for his betrayal. Seeing her sad and broken added more fuel to my rapidly building anger and Sarah could feel it.

"Don't give in to hatred, David. Please," she pleaded.

"You got to go now. You got to find them," Mouge said through her tears.

"I'm coming with you," Sarah said.

"No, I'm going alone. You stay with Mouge," I answered.

"David, Mouge will be fine. Others will come. Mouge still has many friends. The dead will be buried. Mouge will heal. This place will go on," Mouge said. She struggled and stood to her feet. She was a strong old woman.

"Sarah, stay and find Joshua and Sam," I urged.

Mouge was about to protest again when a change washed over her. Her expression went from one of worry and grief to one of surprise and confusion. She reached out and touched Sarah's face and closed her eyes.

"What is it Mouge?" Sarah asked.

"David be right. Mouge needs you here," The old woman said firmly.

"What did you see, what is it?" Sarah asked again.

"Nothin', Mouge just not thinking right. David be right. Listen to 'im. Mouge needs you," she said with a hint of desperation in her voice.

"Alright, I'll stay. David, be careful. And come back to me. I love you," she said.

"I love you too, Sarah. I never stopped."

I kissed her goodbye and lingered looking into her endless eyes for as long as I dared. With each passing second I imagined the miles between Sonja and I expanding exponentially.

"I have to go now," I said.

"There's a small airstrip on the north side of the island," she said.

I nodded and without another word, I exploded into motion. I tore into the earth with each footstep. Speeding faster and faster toward the airstrip. I pushed my still new body harder than I had ever before and found new limits to my speed. The world I moved in was without motion, frozen in time as I passed through it. I was at my destination moments after I had begun to travel. There was no activity at the airport. If they had come this way then they were already gone. I stood there trying to sort out my next move, unsure how to proceed when I heard someone speak my name in the distance. It was Sam. He was beckoning me to come. He knelt on the ground over someone. I closed the distance between us in almost an instant.

"Are you tryin' ta kill me, mate? That noise ya makin' is gonna blow someone's brains outta their head!" he said, holding his hands over his ears.

"Sorry, Sam. I didn't mean to," I answered.

"No worries. I'm fine. Just a little ringin'," he replied.

Joshua lay unconscious in the grass just off the tarmac.

"What happened to him?" I asked.

"He's alive but he's hurt bad. See, me an him, we had a bit of trouble last night an, well I might of turned him into a werewolf without him wantin' to be one. Well he ran off and I ran after. I chased him all over this blasted island. He caught the smell of something 'bout the same time I did and he thundered off in this direction. I seen him run out here. And I seen the others. I held back here on the edge of the forest. I was too far behind 'im to stop 'im from runnin' out there. I didn't see them other kids in the plane at first. I just seen Sonja and Lorelei standin outside the plane. He was full on wolf when he started runnin' to 'em. Course they didn't respond to well ta that. But he figured out how ta shift back to 'imself before he got to 'em. Sonja welcomed him with open arms like a long lost dog. Then snap. She twisted his head like it was nothing and threw em over here."

"They climbed into the plane and off they went. I caught sight of them other kids as I ran over here. Sonja, she eyed me real good but didn't bother stoppin' to crack my skull. They just took off not ten minutes ago. I been shoutin' for help but there's not a soul round here," Sam said.

"Can you fly a plane?" I asked hurriedly.

"Yeah, mate. I can fly a bit but what 'bout 'im. I was scared ta move 'im at all. He's breathin' but I was scared his neck was broken an I can't wake 'im and if he didn't wake up after the thunder you made then he ain't wakin' up," Sam said.

"We have to get him to a hospital. I'll get help," I said as I turned to go back to the place where Mouges home once stood.

"Easy, easy! Nice and slow ta start," Sam said. "Me ears are still ringin'," he added.

I waited until I had reached the edge of the forest before I ran full out. Again the living world halted before me and let me pass with an almost undetectable passage of time. I found Sarah and Mouge very much as I had left them and they were both surprised to see me return so quickly.

"It's Joshua, he's hurt badly. His neck may be broken. Sam is with him. They're at the airport. Sonja's gone. Sam saw them leave on a charter plane. Sam said he can fly. I'm going to follow her, " I said.

"I'll be back, Mouge. I'll get Joshua to the hospital and I'll come back," Sarah said.

"Mouge be fine. You go on now." Mouge replied.

"Let me carry you," I said. "I seem to be getting faster."

"I noticed when you left before, my ears are still ringing."

"I'll start slow," I said as I scooped her into my arms.

In seconds the vivid landscape became a snap shot with the two of us as its only animated inhabitants. The journey back took less than seconds and it was difficult to judge the remaining distance in order to slow down before coming to a stop. My body would tolerate the sudden jolt but the Sarah's body, the werewolf in human form, was just as fragile as any mortal. Our sudden appearance startled Sam as we had not been visible until I slowed to a stop, only meters from him.

"Sam c'mon, Sarah is going to take care of Joshua. We have to hurry if we have any hope of catching her," I said.

"Right, mate. I'm on it," Sam replied as he hurried off to the only hanger at the deserted airport. Sarah began checking Joshua's injuries.

"David, there's a radio in the hanger, call for help," she said.

I moved almost instantly to the entrance of the large hanger door. Moving in that manner was becoming second nature. Sam stood just inside the doorway, before I could question him as to why he was just standing there I saw the reason for his statue like gaze. The small airport had not been deserted. There were what appeared to be several people strewn around the hanger.

"Sam, Sam, go back outside. I'll bring the plane out, "I said. "Sam!" I shouted, snapping him out of his frozen state.

"Right, Okay," he managed to say as he slowly backed out the door.

I went to the radio and began calling for emergency assistance. I managed to reach the islands rescue squad and got an ambulance in route. It was easy enough to pull the twin engine plane from the hanger. It seemed to weigh very little. It was the first heavy object I had attempted to move since becoming a vampire and I couldn't help but marvel at the ease with which I accomplished the task. Once outside I checked to make sure Sam was alright and he began making preparations for flight.

I told Sarah about the grizzly scene inside the hanger and it wounded her deeply. She knew most of the inhabitants of the island and all but a few were werewolf kind. By the time Sam had readied the plane, sirens could be heard in the distance. I kissed her goodbye. She gave Sam the approximate path and distance to the nearest large aircraft airport on the mainland. We climbed aboard and taxied down the runway.

I hated leaving Sarah behind me. I was terrified that she would somehow cease to exist outside my presence. I wasn't sure if we were heading in the right direction, or if they were even heading to the mainland. The airplane moved so slowly I wished that I could move through the air as quickly as I move on land. My mind was racing. My thoughts were shifting from Sarah to Eden to Ann and the other children.

That's my child, I kept telling myself. But it seemed a lie even when I said it out loud. *He is so much more than that,* I thought to myself. *He is something this world has never seen. A being that requires nothing. He has no want for anything,* I marveled to myself. *He grows more and more every day. And he healed Mouge. What does it all mean? What are the dreams? What do they mean? Am I losing my mind? I just need to calm down. I just need to relax.* I told myself.

***

I'd been through this enough to know what was going on. I could see him sitting on a stool in front of an easel, about thirty yards from where I was standing. He was dabbing bits of paint on a canvas as he looked out over a large river valley. It was the same old man I'd seen before. I ran to him. Not as a vampire would run but as a man. It felt strange moving in such a human manner.

"I have to know. Who are you?" I asked.

"I am many things, in many worlds, but then you already know that," he replied as he continued to dab paint on the canvas.

"I don't understand," I said. "I don't understand any of this. Please help me understand," I pleaded.

"A picture, David, as they say, is worth a thousand words," he replied as he lifted the canvas from the easel and placed it in my hands.

***

A pocket of turbulent air jolted me awake.

"You alright, mate? Sam asked, looking back at me over his shoulder.

"I'm fine, I think," I replied.

"Well, I was just thinking that if you wanted ta tear the plane apart, that ya might wait 'til were on the ground," he added.

I didn't understand for a moment but I realized very quickly that I had torn the arm rests of the chair.

"Sorry, Sam," I said.

"Yea, if ya don't mind, I'd prefer ya stay awake for the rest a the flight," he replied with a cautious grin.

"Agreed," I replied. I was shaken. I couldn't get the image on the old man's canvas out of my mind. It seemed the further I went the more complex the answers became and I was getting the sense that this was all part of a much bigger picture of which I could only see a small part. It wasn't a painting at all. It was like looking back to the beginning of time and billions of years flashed before me in an instant. My mind still struggled to comprehend what I had seen.

I saw today, yesterday, last week, last month, last year, ten, a hundred, a thousand, millions of years race by. I was beginning to understand who or what he was for the first time but I couldn't quite put it into words just yet. We landed at Vancouver International Airport but we were able to determine that the only private plane that had been chartered that day was bound for the eastern seaboard, more specifically, Rhode Island international airport. Sam and I chartered our own plane and began the long flight east. I picked up a pen and a small notebook at the gift shop, I felt suddenly compelled to journal the events that led me to this moment in time.

If my dreams mean anything, and I feel now that they do, then it's important to me, that someone, someday read my tale. Though my destiny is not yet fulfilled and the end has yet to be written, this is the story of how I came to be. And the course I have followed until now. I am, David Cross, Vampire.

T. S. Worley

Our story continues...

Coming soon in your favorite bookstore!

T. S. Worley

About the Author

T.S. Worley, author of an exciting new vampire saga, is pleased to be a recent addition to the World Castle Publishing family. His debut novel, entitled "CROSS" was completed in the author's mind more than twenty years ago before ever putting pen to paper. In June 2009 the project officially began thanks to the spark given to him by a dedicated writer by the name of Coleen Baker. The second book in the saga as well as two other novels is currently under way with the flame of writing fully kindled. T.S. Worley currently works in the field of psychiatric medicine and resides in East Tennessee, nestled in a small town on the Cumberland Plateau with the love of his life and children.